Follow Me!

(I'm Lost)

I0567240

The Tale of an Unexpected Leader

A Parable by
Wayne Visser

Paperback edition first published in 2019
by Kaleidoscope Futures
Glebe Farm Cottage, Narford Road, Narborough PE32 1 HZ, UK

Cover image and book illustrations by Laura G. Lugo.

ISBN 978-1-908875-36-5

12 Unconventional Leadership Lessons

1. To find your path, you must lose your way

2. To lead others, you must follow yourself

3. To have a vision, you must close your eyes

4. To have a following, you must walk away

5. To give direction, you must stand in one place

6. To be at the front, you must stay behind

7. To move forward, you must go round in circles

8. To be clearly heard, you must be quiet

9. To embrace the future, you must let go of the past

10. To find the shoots, you must know your roots

11. To fly the highest, you must clip your wings

12. To learn how to lead, you must forget what you know

The Tale of an Unexpected Leader

Unconventional Leadership Lesson #1

TO FIND YOUR PATH, YOU MUST LOSE YOUR WAY

There was no denying it any longer. Gulliver, son of the brave Scottish goose, Gilgamesh, of the clan Scoraig, was lost – on his way to leadership school. He was a failed leader even before he began. How could he, let alone his proud parents or anyone else, have believed that one day he would lead the flock? He couldn't even lead himself from their remote home on Little Loch Broom to the British Academy of Ghans Leadership in London.

Gulliver was gliding, a freeze-frame of feathery form silhouetted against a fading sky in which dusk was rapidly descending. His outstretched neck was taut, his head turning from side to side, his eyes cast downward, straining to spot something familiar in the landscape – a jagged edge of a famous rocky outcrop, the shapely curve of a remembered forest edge, the patchwork blotches of a timeless marshy wetland – frankly, anything that would give him a clue to where he was. One thing was for certain; it was not London, where he was meant to be. And yet, even as he searched, he already knew the truth. He had known it for several hours now, but he didn't want to admit defeat. 'Failure,' he recalled his stern father saying, 'is *not* an option'. Except now, it seemed, it actually was. Success may be hard to achieve. But Gulliver was discovering that failure – or at least admitting failure – was hard too. He could already hear the mocking taunts of his schoolmates – 'Did you hear about gormless Gulliver? You know, the stray Scot from Scoraig? The one who got lost – *on his first day of leadership school!* Honk! Honk! Honk!'

As the sun was setting, Gulliver decided that he should find somewhere to land and rest for the night. But everywhere he looked, there was endless, undulating nothingness. Nothing. Nothing. Nothing. Just stretches of rolling, ribbed sand. And more sand. And more sand, now turning a shadowy shade of rouge against the crimson sky. At last, just as he was losing hope of ever finding a sheltered spot in the desolate landscape, and just as his strength was starting to fail, he saw a cluster of trees in the distance. At least, he *thought* they were trees. He wasn't sure because, like the sandy desert, they were nothing like anything he had ever seen before. They seemed to sprout from the sand like giant reeds, with bare trunks, covered in jagged scales. And the leaves, if indeed they were leaves, were like feathers sticking out of the top of the tree trunks. They reminded him a bit of a peacock's crown.

Gulliver landed in a spray of fine, golden dust, stumbling and ending up beak-first in the sand. It was very undignified. Like rubbing salt in the wound of his already injured pride. Luckily, he was alone and was spared the embarrassment of an audience. Thank Gander for small mercies.

'Hello,' said a raspy voice behind him.

Gulliver nearly jumped out of his gooseflesh and moulted on the spot, landing, once again, beak-first in the sand. His composure was already beyond saving, but when he at least regained his webbed feet, Gulliver craned his neck skyward and honked, flustered and rather rudely: 'Hello yourself!'

The strange looking beast seemed unphased by Gulliver's lack of manners; her narrow, quizzical face, big eyes and unbelievably long eyelashes all remained unmoved and impassive. 'How are you?'

Gulliver heard his mother, Glynnis, honking wildly in his mind's ear. Then, not satisfied with a verbal scolding, she also poked him in his mind's eye, wagging her head with disapproval at his ill-mannered behaviour. Gulliver ignored her. 'I'm terrible. But that's not the question.'

The stranger's lopsided lips slackened like an overstretched elastic band, in what may have been a grin. 'What *is* the question?'

'The question,' honked Gulliver, still indignant with embarrassment, 'is not *how* I am, but rather *where* I am?'

'And where do you think you are?'

7

'Oh, I see, that's how you're going to play it. I bet you think you're *so* clever now?'

The stranger chuckled, unconsciously blowing little bubbles with her rubbery lips. 'Of course I'm Clever. But how did you know? I am Cuthbert, the Clever Camel, of the Cleopatra Caravan. And this is the Sahara desert.'

Gulliver wasn't sure if he was being teased and should retort angrily, but before he could decide, he was distracted by something else. He had just noticed that Cuthbert had a gigantic hump on his back! Gulliver was fascinated. And confused. And curious. And tongue-tangled. He didn't know what to ask first. He forgot all about his fatigue, and his thirst, and his hunger; even his shame. All his questions tumbled out at once.

'Is-that-a-hump-where-is-the-Sahara-what's-a-desert-can-you-blow-big-bubbles-too?'

Cuthbert laughed a deep, throaty laugh, causing his lips to dance and his hump to jiggle. Despite his best efforts, Gulliver couldn't help himself – he laughed too. Cuthbert recovered first and spoke, more softly and gently this time: 'Let's start at the beginning, shall we? *How* you are is always more important than *where* you are. So, why are you unhappy?'

Gulliver opened his beak to speak, then closed it. He opened it again, and closed it again. This was new! Never before in Gulliver's ten-year life had he ever been speechless. He tried to analyse why he was lost for words. Was it that he didn't have an answer? Did he really have nothing to say? No, that wasn't it. If anything, he had too much to say. Where would he start? But that wasn't it either. Finally, it dawned on him. He was simply flabbergasted into silence because nobody – not his parents, nor his five siblings; not his grandparents (when they were still alive), nor his school teachers – nobody had ever asked him whether he was unhappy, let alone why.

Gulliver tried again, and this time, words came out of his beak, slowly and hesitantly at first, but then steadily and soon they were gushing in a waterfall of words. 'I should be happy,' he began apologetically. 'I have nothing to complain about really. I have good parents, a good home, a good education. In fact, I am from a very well respected family in a very well respected flock in a place called Scoraig . . . which is a peninsular in Scotland,' he added helpfully.

'I see.' Cuthbert nodded and patiently waited for Gulliver to continue.

'In fact, my father is Chief Navigator of the Scoraig Flock, and my mother is a Senior Slug Forager. Of course, my father expects me to follow in his webprints and be the Flock's next great navigator. Which is why he sent me to Leadership School down in London. Which is where I'm meant to be. Which I'm not.'

'I see,' nodded Cuthbert. 'And you're unhappy *because* ... ?'

Gulliver began to think that Cuthbert maybe wasn't so clever after all. Maybe he was just named Cuthbert the Clever, in the same way that Oxford Circus wasn't really a circus and Covent Gardens wasn't really a garden. Oh well, he'd just have to spell it out for the crazy camel.

'I'm unhappy ...' he paused and sighed deeply for dramatic effect. 'Because I'm ... I'm LOST!' Gulliver almost choked on the word, and it came out as a splutter.

Cuthbert laughed. And he laughed. And he laughed.

Gulliver was shocked. He frowned. And he scowled.

'Isn't *everybody*?' gasped Cuthbert, still breathless from laughing.

'Isn't everybody *what*?' exclaimed Gulliver, exasperated now.

'Lost!' said Cuthbert. 'Isn't everybody lost?'

Gulliver had never met a camel before, so he didn't know what camels did. But he was beginning to think that he was looking to the wrong species for advice.

'You don't understand,' cried Gulliver. 'I'm a goose. Geese migrate. Everything we are taught leads up to the Great Migration. What's more, my family have been the Chief Navigators for generations. Our reputation and the reputation of all the great ganders in the sky is built on always knowing where we are. We are never lost. Never! Do you understand? No, of course, how could you. You're not a goose. You don't migrate.'

'Well, that may be true,' nodded Cuthbert, still placid. 'And that may be not quite true.'

Gulliver threw him a quizzical, challenging look.

'We don't exactly migrate,' continued Cuthbert. 'But we do go on long journeys across the desert.'

Gulliver had no idea, but he wasn't going to let his new friend placate him so easily. 'Well, then you *should* know the importance of navigation. You *should* know that it's critical to have a flight path (or in your case a footpath), and to be able, at any moment, to plot where you are along the route. And you *should* know that knowledge of these paths is passed down from grandfather to father to son. The Wisdom of the Flock keeps us from ever being lost in the eternal skies. The important thing is that we are *never* lost or off our bearings, like I am now.'

For the first time, Cuthbert looked serious; maybe even confused. 'On the contrary,' he mused. '*We* only know the importance of moving forward. We never know exactly where we are, but we always know that we are moving in the right direction. Any paths that our ancestors may have trod are long since covered by the shifting dunes of the desert. The Wisdom of the Caravan teaches that we are all lost in the vast oceans of sand. The important thing is not that we are found, but that we are moving together.'

Gulliver's head was spinning. He could feel the fatigue of a full day's flying starting to weigh down on him, like a poacher's heavy net. And yet, he felt that somewhere at the edge of his weariness and confusion, there lay a great lesson in leadership, if only he could grasp it. He needed to understand how camels could travel thousands of miles together and still be lost.

'But how do you know you're moving in the right direction, if there is no plan, and you don't know where you are and there are no paths and everyone is lost?' Gulliver sounded every bit as bewildered as he felt.

'We know where we are going,' replied Cuthbert, slowly and deliberately. 'Because we know who we are. We know our true nature and this guides us to our invisible goal.' He could see the travel-weary bird was struggling to grasp what he was saying, so he tried again. 'It is in a camel's nature to thirst for water and to long for shade. By listening to our inner desire, we sense whether we are moving closer or further away from quenching our spirit.'

This was heady-stuff and Gulliver's head already felt like it was clogged with sand. He had never heard the Flock talk about 'sensing' and 'desires' and 'spirit'. Was it really possible to be guided by some sort of inner compass? He knew his parents would berate him for such heretical ideas. He could almost hear the Flock honking their derision. But even as Gulliver's head became heavy and the compulsion to tuck it under his wing became almost irresistible, he felt that something had shifted in him.

True, he was lost. But so what? For some strange, inexplicable reason, it didn't seem to matter as much as it had a few hours before. Accepting this new, liberating possibility, Gulliver felt himself relax and his head gently dropped, nuzzling into his soft, downy feathers. The last thing he remembered hearing, as he slipped into a deep, rejuvenating sleep, was his crazy, clever friend Cuthbert saying in a soothing voice:

'Gulliver, my newfound feathered friend, don't be sad any longer. As my aunt Christine always used to say: To find your path, you must lose your way'.

Unconventional Leadership Lesson #2

To LEAD OTHERS, YOU MUST FOLLOW YOURSELF

Gulliver woke with a beak full of sand. He was about to spit with disgust and sigh with despair, but then he remembered his crazy encounter with Cuthbert. And so, instead, he found himself smiling (to the extent that geese can smile). The fog of a dream was just fading from memory. In the dream, he had been flying over a great lake, as big as the ocean, and looking down, he saw not just his own reflection, but hundreds of other geese, all flying in a grand-V formation behind him.

He shook his head, looked around and saw nothing but a lake of burnt-umber sand. Cuthbert was nowhere to be seen, and despite the early hour and the shade under the palm trees, Gulliver was already feeling the heat. Then he remembered that he was lost. Panic rose up from the pit of his stomach and caught in his throat. But just as quickly the crazy, clever camel's words echoed in his head and the panic subsided. 'It is okay to be lost, so long as ...' What had Cuthbert said? 'So long as you are moving in the right direction.' That was it.

'Well, Gulliver,' the lost goose asked himself aloud. 'Are you moving in the right direction?' The question suddenly seemed simple. He knew he had been flying south west when he got lost. So, logically, the right direction – the way back to London and leadership school and home – must be north east. He checked the position of the sun, turned to face north east, and stretched his wings, preparing for takeoff. That was easy, he thought.

'Maybe too easy?' The rebellious thought had strayed across his mental horizon just as he was leaning forward to start his pre-flight run-up.

Gulliver frowned. Too easy? Why had he unexpectedly thought that? The logic was infallible: when he got lost, he was flying south east from Scoraig to London, so surely to correct his mistake . . .

'What if it wasn't a mistake?'

Gulliver shook his head, irritated. He wasn't used to hearing voices in his head, let alone ones that contradicted himself. Except this voice had a strangely camelish tone, so he decided not to dismiss it quite so quickly. After all, what had Cuthbert said about knowing the right direction? He had talked about a camel's true nature and innate desires and spirit. Gulliver ignored what felt like a sandstorm in his brain and tried to apply the unexpected leadership lesson he'd learned the previous night.

I am a barnacle goose. So what is my true gander nature? What are my most goosely desires? Where is the spirit of the Flock leading me?

These were profound and perplexing questions, and Gulliver's nut-sized brain started to hurt. He waited for a great revelation – a flash of light or an unmistakable sign from the Great Gander in the Sky – but he saw nothing. He heard no answers to the big questions. Maybe it was because he was distracted by feeling so hot and dusty and thirsty. Forget the philosophising, he thought. What I want is somewhere cooler. I want to feel the ocean breeze. I want to taste the salty air and to skim on the water and to plunge my feet into its cool depths.

Just then, Gulliver felt a slight movement of the baking air and smelled – no, it was more subtle than that – he *sensed* that it was a sea breeze. If he just took off into the breeze, roughly south-east, he was certain he would find the sea. Something inside him told him he was right, that this was the right direction to fly. And before he could second-guess himself, he had taken off and was heading further away from everything he knew and loved and missed. He was flying away from home.

Strangely, Gulliver wasn't sad or worried. On the contrary, it felt good to be flying again. More than that, he felt a twinge of excitement knowing that he was heading straight into the unknown.

Below, as Gulliver flew, the landscape began changing, with the yellow shifting sand dunes giving way to dry rocky brown desert. After an hour, he flew over a great river, flanked with strip-lungs of green. Flying low and slow, he noticed ancient buildings carved into the cliffs on the river bank, with images of giant human kings etched into their facades. It was tempting to rest in the shade of these great temples and to try and decipher the scratchings on their pillars and walls, but the desire for the cool ocean was more compelling, so he flew on. After another hour, Gulliver reached a range of majestic mountains and his heart lifted with hope. As the colours changed from brown to green, he was able to ride the thermals, rising up in circles until he could clear the peaks. To his immense relief and honking joy, he could see the ocean stretched out, in the distance, refreshingly blue and immense.

When Gulliver finally made it to the sea, he made a point of executing an exaggerated ski-landing, revelling in the cool salty spray and shaking his feathers with a feeling of jubilation that he had never felt before in his life. After several minutes of unadulterated splashing and shaking and ducking and diving and honking and hooting, Gulliver calmed down enough to realise that he was famished and exhausted. Having grown up on a peninsula, it didn't take him long to locate a good feeding spot, blooming with seaweed and algae. He ate his fill and, feeling refreshed, decided to explore a little.

Looking at the coastline, as he bobbed up and down, Gulliver could see that it was drier and sandier than his home in Scotland. He wondered where he was. What was south-east of Egypt? His geography lessons at school had only taught him northern lands, along the Flock's annual migration path. He wondered whether his fish friends would be different in this part of the world as well. So he stuck his head under the water and looked around. He got his answer soon enough, as two blue-grey shadows glided towards him – one large and one small.

In a great fluster of feathers and squawking, Gulliver leapt into the air and flew out of the jaws of certain death. Or at least, that's what he thought at first. He was old enough to know about sharks and he wasn't taking any chances! Of course, he knew about dolphins too, but as his mother always repeated, *ad nauseam*: 'Safety first! Bravery is no good if you're someone else's breakfast'.

Having regained his breath and lowered his pulse, Gulliver circled back around to check on the danger he had narrowly escaped. On closer inspection, the drifting shadows didn't fit the profile of either sharks or dolphins. His curiosity was piqued. He wanted to find out more, but should he take the chance?

In the end, intrigue triumphed over fear, and the two shadows rose to the surface nearby. Gulliver couldn't help but stare. He was looking at a face that was nothing like he'd ever seen before. Staring back at him were small black eyes, set on a smooth grey head, with a bump for a nose and a snout that looked distinctly funnel-ish.

'Hello', said the kindly face, 'I'm Daphne, and this is my son, Dodger'.

Gulliver remembered his manners. 'Hello, I'm Gulliver and I'm . . . ' He was going to say lost, but the word stuck in his throat. Instead he said, 'I'm searching.'

He expected the placid creature to say, 'Searching for what?' (which would be problematic, because he didn't really know). But instead she said, 'What a wonderful coincidence! So are we!'

'What are *you* searching for?' said Gulliver, relieved to turn the question around.

'We're searching for a new home for our school.' He saw Dodger nodding, a little sadly.

'I left my home too,' said Gulliver. 'To go to Leadership School. What kind of school is yours?'

'Well,' said Daphne gently. 'We're the Dugongs of Djibouti. Some call us the women of the sea, because sailors used to think we were mermaids. Be that as it may, we live in schools, like fish. Our school is like your flock, although those with less respect call us sea cows and say we live in herds.'

Gulliver blushed, feeling stupid. Of course he knew fish swam in schools. It's just that his new friends didn't really look like fish, or dolphins, or whales for that matter. To mask his embarrassment, he quickly asked, 'What's wrong with your old home?'

'It's being destroyed,' piped up Dodger, adding indignantly, 'by human beans!'

'Human *beings*', corrected his mother patiently. 'But it is true. Our habitat is being destroyed by Man's greed for fish, his polluting factories and poisonous farms, not to mention his hunting as a sport. Humans hunt us for our meat and our oil. Not only that, but now the

19

ocean is warming up and becoming more acidic and our sea-grass is dying or growing in different places. Still, we mustn't complain . . . ' Her voice trailed off with the blue ripples of the ocean water.

'There are only 50 of us left,' said Dodger plaintively. 'Off the coast of Africa,' he added, somehow guessing that Gulliver wasn't quite sure where he was.

Gulliver didn't know what to say. It was such a sad story. Suddenly, *his* problems – like getting lost and missing his home and his friends and his family – didn't seem nearly so bad. There was an awkward silence. He searched his tiny brain for something appropriate to say. In the end, all that came out of his beak was, 'So where is the rest of your school?'

'They're waiting for us,' squeaked Dodger, suddenly more cheerful. 'We're the leaders!'

'That is true,' nodded Daphne. 'We're the advance scouts.'

Gulliver opened his eyes wide. Then a cloud of confusion crossed his face. 'So, you're leaders, but your followers are not with you?' His question petered out in the wind.

'Absolutely!' replied Daphne. 'What is the most important lesson we have learned about leadership?'

Gulliver panicked, but to his relief, he saw that Daphne was looking at Dodger. The juvenile dugong thought for a few seconds and then replied confidently: 'To lead others, you must follow yourself!'

Daphne nodded and smiled a beautiful funnel-shaped smile. 'And what about you then?' She had turned back to Gulliver. 'Are you also an advance scout?'

Gulliver hesitated. He didn't want to lie, but he also didn't want to appear clueless. 'I guess in a way I am, although I'm very new to this scouting business.'

'Don't worry, there's nothing to it,' said Daphne reassuringly. 'All you have to do is follow your bliss. Remember, the school – or the flock in your case – won't always know what it wants, or where to go next. Mostly, they are just happy to stay where they are, even if it kills them. Your job is to look for new paths, new possibilities, new futures. And' she added, looking straight into his eyes, 'sometimes you can only do that alone.'

It made a lot of sense, the way Daphne put it. Maybe his navigational *faux pas* could turn into something good; not only an adventure for himself, but a new home for his beloved, belligerent flock.

'So where to next?' Dodger was looking at him expectantly.

'Well . . . ' said Gulliver slowly, deep in thought. He was still reflecting on Daphne's profound words, and trying to imagine what following himself really meant, now that he was faced with yet another decision. 'The only thing my flock know about is their rock on the peninsula, and flying north for their annual migration. So . . . ' Gulliver was thinking aloud. 'If I'm going to find new flight paths, or even a new home for the Great Flock, I suppose I must fly in the opposite direction. I'm flying south!' concluded Gulliver with a sudden flourish of clarity and confidence.

'Well then, we wish you the best of luck, Gulliver the Gallant Goose,' said Daphne and Dodger waved a little flipper.

Gulliver couldn't help but fluff his feathers a little bit. Did she really say *gallant* goose? Could it be true? He saw they were about to dive back under the waves, so he hastily said his goodbyes. 'I hope you find a lovely new home. And thank you for the lesson in leadership'. He watched as their tails disappeared, feeling at the same time melancholic and euphoric. With fresh resolve, he gave himself a little pep-talk: Gallant Gulliver, time waits for no bird, so onwards and southwards!

Unconventional Leadership Lesson #3

TO HAVE A VISION, YOU MUST CLOSE YOUR EYES

Gulliver took off heading due south, which quickly took him away from the shoreline, heading inland. Although he didn't know it yet, he was flying across the horn of Africa and into Ethiopia. The landscape below him rose steadily, then pushed up dramatically into a range of snow-capped peaks. It was higher than Gulliver had ever flown in his life and he was exhilarated.

As he flew, he pondered his strange encounter with the gentle Dugongs of Djibouti – such fabulous creatures, why would humans want to destroy them, or take away their home? Could they not see their beauty? Could they not sense their great wisdom? Could they not respect their peaceful ways?

Of course, it was not the first time he had heard stories of Man's destructiveness. His mother had taught him early on that humans are cruel and insensitive creatures – predators, like foxes and owls, only worse. His great grandfather had been killed by a human. He was shot down from the sky when the Great Flock had just started its migration north. Gulliver didn't really understand how guns worked, but he knew they were deadly. Worse still, wherever there are humans, there are those great menaces – dogs and cats, both of which seemed to think that 'goose' was just another word for 'lunch'. So he knew humans were to be avoided at all costs. But what did they have against the beautiful Dugongs?

Gulliver's head began to hurt. Maybe it was an overdose of pondering, or maybe it was the altitude. The air was thin, crisp and cool. Just then, he was cresting the mountain tops. He landed on a rock, stopping for a rest and puffing his feathers out against the icy wind. His head started to clear and he marvelled at the spectacular view across the plains, stretching out below him all the way to the horizon. At that moment, he wished his family and friends were with him. What would they say about such grandeur? It was nothing like home. And it was exquisite.

Gulliver set off again and for the next few hours, flying was easy as he glided down from the mountains to the vast open plains. By the time the sun began to set, the landscape had changed from the rocky, green, forested highlands to tufted, brown, sandy lowlands. Gulliver spotted a little clump of bushes, landed and nestled down. Exhaustion quickly overtook him and he drifted off to sleep.

Some hours later, Gulliver was woken up by a scratching sound. He blinked open his eyes and cast about for the source of disturbance. The moon was nearly full, so it was easy to see, but he didn't spot anything suspicious. Even so, the dull scratching sound continued. He cocked his head and tried to locate which direction it was coming from. 'That's strange,' he thought. 'It seems to be coming from below me.'

Gulliver was wide awake now, so he decided to investigate. It didn't take him long to discover that he was surrounded by a vast network of holes that burrowed into the earth. His mother had warned him that sometimes foxes or snakes can live in holes, so he wasn't about to stick his head in one to find out more.

Luckily, he didn't have to, because just then a head popped out of one of the burrows nearby. Or at least, he assumed it was a head. In fact, it was the strangest thing he had ever seen in his life – and that's saying a lot, given his recent encounters with stranger-than-strange Cuthbert, Daphne and Dodger! Its face – Gulliver had decided it *must* be a face – consisted almost entirely of two massive teeth. Behind these, on either side, he could just make out a twitching nose and two small screwed up eyes, almost closed. More strangely still, its skin was pinky-grey and wrinkled, with no trace of hair or fur or feathers.

'Could you please keep it down up here!'

Gulliver was startled by the small, high pitched voice, sounding distinctly irritated. 'I beg your pardon?' Gulliver retorted.

'You're making a heck of a racket, and some of us are trying to sleep; others are working the night shift.'

'A heck of a racket? I was asleep!'

'Well, in that case, you were honking in your sleep.'

Gulliver's indignation dissolved in an instant. 'Was I really?'

'Yes, you were. Bad dream?' Gulliver noted a hint of sympathy in its voice.

'Yes, I suppose it was,' said Gulliver, as the misty shape of his dream drifted in front of his mind's eye. 'I dreamt that I was trying to convince the Elders of the Great Flock to change their migration path, to fly south instead of north, so that they could see the wonders of Africa, like I've seen. But they would have none of it. They told me to shut my beak. Can you believe it? They told me it was blasphemy to even suggest changing the ancient ways of the Great Goose in the Sky.'

Gulliver was shaking his head vigorously, still swept up in the emotional storm of his dream. The toothy creature, on the other hand, was impassive: gazing at him, chewing on some invisible delicacy, not saying anything. 'He must think I'm terribly rude,' thought Gulliver.

'I'm sorry,' Gulliver continued. 'I didn't properly introduce myself. I'm Gulliver, of the Great Flock of Geese in Scoraig, Scotland.

I'm on an unexpected adventure, and I've never been to this beautiful land before. To be honest, I've never seen some . . . thing as . . . '. Gulliver coughed involuntarily. 'Something as *special* as yourself.'

The creature seemed unphased. 'Well, Sir Gulliver, my name is Roody, of the Snuggly Nest of Naked Mole Rats in Ginir, Ethiopia. And I don't know much about migration paths. Unless, by some chance, they are like tunnels. I know *all* about tunnels: long tunnels, short tunnels, curvy tunnels, squiggly tunnels, tunnels that go up and tunnels that go down, tunnels that never end and tunnels that are a dead end. Yes sir, Mister Gulliver, I know tunnels!'

Gulliver couldn't help but show a beaky smile. 'As it happens, Roody, migrant paths *are* a bit like tunnels, except they're up in the sky, not down in the earth.'

'Well then, in *that* case, I know what your problem is.'

'My problem?'

'Yes, what you did wrong in your dream.'

'Oh, *that* problem. What did I do wrong?'

'Well, it so happens – I don't know if I mentioned this – it so happens that I am an expert on tunnels. Not just an expert, mind you. I am the Master Tunnel Builder for my nest of 80 mole rats. But I wasn't always the Master Builder. Do you know what I was before I was the Master Builder?'

'Umm, no, I don't.' Gulliver thought it best not to interrupt Roody's flow.

'Before I was a Master Builder, I was an Apprentice. That's because my father was the Master Tunnel Builder, and you can't have more than one Master at a time. Are you following me?'

Gulliver nodded.

'Now, what is the first lesson you learn as an Apprentice?'

Gulliver couldn't even begin to guess. But he did anyway. 'How to dig?'

'How to dig? How to *dig*!? No, no, no! Where did you get such a feather-brained idea from? How to dig, well I never! No, the first lesson you learn as an Apprentice is *what to dig for*. It's no good just digging for the sake of digging now is it? There's no point in building beautiful tunnels that just go round in circles now is it?'

Gulliver felt that 'stupid' feeling creeping over him again. He shook his head timidly. 'No', he squeaked, almost inaudibly.

'And what do we dig for?'

Gulliver wasn't going to fall for that trick again. 'I really don't know'.

Roody seemed pleased with Gulliver's ignorance, and took great pride in enlightening him. 'We dig for the grand prize, don't we? Not the *little* prize. Not the *teeny weenie* prize. Not the *insignificant* prize. Not the *prize that the other mole rats wouldn't even consider a prize*. The *grand* prize. Do you catch my drift?'

Gulliver wasn't sure he did, but he nodded anyway. Then Roody changed tack, confusing him even further.

'Do you think mole rats *enjoy* munching their way through dirt every day and every night?'

Gulliver tried to imagine himself eating sand 24 hours a day and the answer seemed obvious. Even so, his confidence was battered and shaky, so he made sure to include a question mark in his reply, just in case it was wrong. 'No?'

'No!' squealed Roody, his voice rising in pitch. 'Of *course* they don't!' And yet, they do it. Why? I'm asking you straight, Sir Gulliver, why do they do it?'

There was no wriggling out of this one. Sensing that there must be some logic to Roody's convoluted rant, he ventured: 'Because of the big prize?'

'Exactly! Bravo! Hey presto! Jolly good show! Because of the big prize, precisely!' Roody's anaemic fleshy head seemed about to pop with joy.

Gulliver still wasn't sure he understood, but he was relieved not to have got another answer wrong. Fortunately, Roody didn't ask another question right then. He had obviously decided that Gulliver had earned the right to be trusted with their great secret.

'Mole rats eat dirt because they believe in the Holy Tuber!' He paused, looking expectant. Seeing Gulliver's nonplussed expression, Roody continued. 'What we live for, you see, is tubers. Tubers are succulent, delicious, crunchy, delectable, juicy roots. They are what we eat. Don't get me wrong. We can stay alive eating small bulbs and thin stringy roots. But what we *live* for are fat, fabulous tubers. That's what keeps us all digging in the dirt. And do you know what we do when we find the Holy Tuber – that fattest, most fabulous tuber in all the earth?'

Oh dear, more questions. Gulliver sighed, but he was genuinely interested to know. He decided to stick with the obvious. 'You eat it?'

'Yes, of course we eat it. Well, naturally we eat it. Tubers are for eating after all. But that's not what we *do* with it. There's a secret I'm going to tell you. Can you keep a secret?'

Finally, a question Gulliver knew the answer to. 'Absolutely, I am the best keeper of secrets in the whole Great Flock. Once, my friend Grantham told me . . . '

Roody interrupted him, impatient to share his great hidden truth. 'We don't eat *all* of it!'

Roody was beaming with a smile, his teeth completely hiding his face, as if he had just found the Sacred Writing Quill of the Great Goose herself. But Gulliver didn't get it. So they didn't eat all of it, so what? In the flock, they didn't eat all of the weeds or grass or algae either. So what?

Roody came to the rescue. 'When we find the Holy Tuber, which, I'll have you know, can weigh as much as a thousand times what we weigh, we only eat the inside. Do you get it? We leave the outside, so it keeps growing. The Holy Tuber regenerates. This way, it might even feed us for years!'

Now Gulliver understood. 'That's amazing!' he honked with genuine enthusiasm.

Roody beamed his toothy grin again. 'So your mistake in the dream was . . . ?' Roody was cleverly bringing the conversation back full circle.

Oh dear. In his moment of tuber enlightenment, Gulliver had forgotten how the whole thing got started with Roody. He plutzed and puzzled. He preened and pecked. Roody waited patiently and in silence. Finally, the answer dawned on Gulliver: 'I didn't show the Elders of the Great Flock the grand prize!'

Roody beamed so that all Gulliver could see was his brilliant white teeth flashing in the moonlight. 'Exactly, Sir Gulliver. As my father used to tell me when I was still his Apprentice: "The mole rat masses will only dig for you if you tell them the story of the Quest for the Holy Tuber. To be a Master Builder, my son – to be a true leader – you must create a vision. And to have a vision, you must close your eyes".'

Unconventional Leadership Lesson #4

TO HAVE A FOLLOWING, YOU MUST WALK AWAY

After thanking Roody for his flashes of insight, Gulliver drifted back into a restful, noiseless, dreamless sleep. Then, shortly after sunrise, before it got too hot, he said his goodbyes to Roody and flew off in a south-westerly direction . . . more-or-less. Somehow, precise vectors didn't seem so important anymore. Glancing back, he was sure he could still see Roody's brilliant white teeth flashing in the sun. Gulliver smiled. Such an unexpected meeting – and now he had a nearly blind mole-rat to add to his growing menagerie of strange new friends.

As he flew, Gulliver thought about Roody's lesson in leadership. He wondered what *his* vision was. If the flock were here now, what would he say to inspire them, to convince them that new worlds – better worlds – were waiting to be discovered, if only they would take a chance, if only they would be more courageous? In his head, he could already hear their sniggers and snorts. And he didn't blame them. His vision was still too vague, too much like 'wish-upon-a-star' and not enough like 'follow-that-star!'

He had been flying for hours, lost in a reverie of reflection, but alas, no blinding vision struck him. Then he remembered more precisely what Roody had said: 'To have a vision, you must close your eyes.' *Close your eyes.* Of course! Gulliver slapped his forehead with his wingtip. 'Duh!' he thought. 'I'm such a silly goose,' stalling in mid-air, as if to prove the point. In an undignified blur of feathers and feet, beak and bottom, he eventually regained a level pitch and flew on, hoping no-one had been watching. (Little did he know).

Gulliver decided to try it. He closed his eyes, and the world went black. Actually, no. He had expected it to go black, but it went more orange, with dancing specks of white. 'How strange!' he thought. He decided to experiment a little, and noticed that when he turned his head towards the sun, his inner radar screen went from orange to yellow to almost completely white. And when he turned his head the opposite way, facing almost backwards, it went . . .

'Honk! *Honk!* HONK!'

Gulliver opened his eyes just in time to swerve and avoid a mid-air collision.

'Watch where you're going, you rudderless rat!'

Gulliver glanced back irately to identify the rude source of this belittling barrage of air-rage. When he did, even more than the shock of his near-crash, or the echo of that stinging insult (which was the *worst* kind of insult . . . 'no offense intended to Roody and his family', he quickly thought) – far more surprising was the fact that he was seeing another goose. And not just one goose, but a whole flock. In point of fact, not just a whole flock, but a massive flock – quite possibly as many as fifty glorious geese, all gleaming in the bright noon-day sun.

Gulliver hadn't spotted a single, solitary goose (not even on the horizon) for days and days, let alone a flock in perfect military formation. 'Not since he left home, bound for leadership school in London,' he reflected wistfully. And so it was hardly surprising that his spontaneous burst of joy at seeing a bunch of fellow feathered friends completely extinguished the anger that might have erupted under different circumstances. Gulliver was known to be a feisty flyer in the flock, and was always getting into noisy squabbles with what he thought of as 'less accomplished aeronauts.'

Gulliver's disaster avoidance manoeuvre – 'which was rather skilfully and deftly executed,' he thought with a pinprick of pride in his chest – had taken him up above the flock. Now he looked down and admired their perfect V-formation. And suddenly, he felt terribly homesick. Fortunately (or unfortunately), at that very moment, he heard something – a whisper from below, floating up on the breeze:

'Did you see that? He was flying forwards while looking backwards!' It was one of the birds near the back of the V.

'Not only that. I swear his eyes were closed. Completely shut! I saw it myself,' said the goose positioned one ahead.

'And did you notice,' said a third goose, bringing up the rear. 'He was different. He was not like us at all!'

As Gulliver listened to the gossiping geese below, he felt his newfound joy deflating like a balloon. Sadly, it seemed, his new flock of friends were not so friendly after all. 'How dare they call me a rudderless rat!' The fresh memory flared back into consciousness, reigniting his anger. 'I would rather be a rat, like my wrinkled friend Roody, than a member of this flock of fff. . . ' A mental image of his mother's stern frown caught him just in time. 'And anyway,' he continued muttering to himself. 'What did they mean, he was different? Different *how*?'

The flock had begun to descend, so Gulliver dropped with them, keeping a tidy distance, and began studying them more carefully. It was true. They looked different to him. While he had a handsome black breast, neck, beak and feet, with a pure white face and variegated underbelly and wings, their beak and feet were red, their face was beige with weird brown blotches around their yellow eyes, and they had a brown back, white shoulders and black wings. 'How strange,' he thought. 'How interesting.'

Gulliver watched, fascinated, as they glided in to land on an enormous lake (called Turkana, although he didn't know that). He decided to keep a cautious distance from the flock, and landed on the shore nearby. Of course, his father had told him stories about their cousins from distant lands, even claiming to have met some who had strayed far from their homes. 'Most were lost,' his father had said. 'But some were rebels, loners, adventure-seekers.' Gulliver remembered the tone of disapproval in his father's voice. How strange that all these years later, *he* – Gulliver, son of his father, Gilgamesh – was now the unwitting lone explorer.

All the while, Gulliver was pacing up and down the shoreline, lost in misty memories, trying hard to dredge up what his father had taught him. The names of these distant relations, which had always sounded so exotic and, frankly, made-up, began to seep into Gulliver's consciousness: the Beans and Brents, the Canadians and Egyptians, the Greylags, the Pink-footed and the White-fronted. Maybe his father's stories were not fiction after all.

Just as Gulliver was wondering which group the nearby noisy, brash flock fell into, there was a sudden, splashing commotion on the lake. The flock rose up in unified panic, flying away and settling back down further from the shore.

'I'm not *that* ugly!' honked Gulliver, at once both irritated and slightly depressed.

'You certainly are *not*,' purred a strange, silky voice behind him.

Gulliver leapt two feet straight up into the air, landed back down awkwardly on one foot and toppled over. Scrambling back to his feet, he turned to face the stranger . . . and nearly fertilised the shore. Standing before him was something so frightening, so fierce-looking, so . . . furry, that Gulliver thought he would malt on the spot.

Then again, maybe he had overreacted. It was not really such a ferocious face after all. It was not even a famished face (which relieved Gulliver even more). It was a kindly, almost cuddly, face, smiling out at him from the centre of a fabulous, flaming yellow-and-black ball of fluff.

'On the contrary,' rumbled the giant fluff-thing. 'You look rather dapper in your monochromatic plumage.'

It would be a lie to say that Gulliver wasn't nervous. He was transfixed by the creature's mouth. More particularly, by the size and number of razor-sharp spikes that beamed back at him, leaving him feeling strangely paralysed. What's more, there was something disturbingly familiar about those rows of flesh-ripping, bone-crunching teeth. Hadn't he seen them somewhere before? No, of course not; how could he have? Just then, a little flashbulb went off in

Gulliver's brain. A fox. A FOX! And not just any fox: a *monster fox* on *steroids*!

Every life-preserving instinct Gulliver possessed kicked in, willing him to flee – to fly away as fast and as far as possible. He could even feel the adrenaline shooting through his wings as he launched into the great escape. So great, in fact, that he would spend countless moonlit evenings telling his grand-geese about it in years to come.

Except that he didn't – escape, that is. In his mind, he had taken off in a flurry of brave flight and swooped over the insolent flock in a show of swift agility that would leave them in no doubt just who was the fastest, finest flyer and who was not.

'What's the matter? Cat got your tongue?' purred the Giant Fox.

Gulliver jerked out of his fantasy and back into his perilous predicament. Then he decided that certain death was no reason to be rude. So he stammered, 'Errr . . . thank you. I mean . . . errr . . . good afternoon. You are rather a fabulous spectacle yourself, Mister Fox.'

The golden creature erupted in a roar of laughter that shook the very shore and – Gulliver noted somewhere at the fringes of his awareness – panicked the flock into a flap once more. 'I am many things,' the furry animal spluttered, still chuckling. 'But a fox is not one of them. Allow me to introduce myself, young gander. My name is Lionel and I am – yes, you guessed it, a round of applause please, thank you, thank you, thank you – a lion!'

Gulliver felt his racing heart begin to slow. 'Lionel may be massive,' he thought. 'And he may be sabre-toothed . . . but I like him. He has a certain style, he has a cheery charm, and he is fiendishly funny.' Gulliver swallowed hard and inclined his head theatrically: 'I am Gulliver and I am – yes, you guessed it, a chorus of honks please, thank you, thank you, thank you – a goose!'

Lionel erupted into another roar of uncontrollable laughter, his shaggy mane seeming to dance like the sparkling rays of the very sun itself. 'So tell me, Gulliver, what's all this about being ugly then?'

'Oh that,' replied Gulliver, suddenly feeling embarrassed and sullen. 'It's nothing. Well, not nothing. It's that flock over there. They were rude to me. They were gossiping about me. They said I'm different. And . . . and all I wanted was to be their friend.' He stared at the sand below his webbed feet. 'It's just that I got lost and I haven't seen another goose for ages and . . .'

Gulliver's eyes began tear up. Lionel nodded, but said nothing, his gold-flecked eyes full of compassion. Gulliver sniffed and continued.

'And I'm supposed to become a flock leader. How can I become a flock leader, when I can't even make new friends? When they reject me even before I have a chance? When all they do is laugh at me and chirp behind my back?'

Lionel nodded briskly, as if he suddenly understood exactly what the problem was. Then he rose up to his full regal height, looked Gulliver straight in the eye, and said in a voice full of authority and wisdom: 'Firstly, young Gulliver, don't let *anyone* tell you whether or not you are a leader; only *you* can tell yourself that. Secondly, different is good; in fact, if you're going to be a leader, being different is essential. Thirdly, who says you can't make new friends? What am I then – the cat's whiskers?'

Gulliver smiled. It was all true. He thought about Cuthbert and Daphne and Dodger and Roody – all new friends he had made. And *they* hadn't rejected him because he was different. In fact, they had loved him for it. Gulliver looked up at Lionel, who was still smiling sternly, and answered, 'You *are* my friend, of course. And I am grateful that you are. In fact,' he added, getting some of his zest back, 'I would far rather be your friend than that stupid flock's friend . . . or your lunch.'

Lionel roared with laughter again, and Gulliver joined in, honking loudly. Then Lionel stopped rather abruptly, as if remembering something that he had forgotten to say. 'Do you know what happens when a young, male lion cub grows up? Do you know what he has to do before he can lead his own pride?'

Gulliver shook his head.

'He has to leave the pride he grew up with. He has to turn his back and walk away. He must go into the wilderness on his own.' Lionel had a distant look in his eyes, as if recalling his own isolation. 'Only after he has learned to survive by himself can he become a leader of others. Only when he has mastered his own nature can he become a master of others. Do you understand?'

Gulliver nodded tentatively. It was yet another unexpected lesson in leadership from an unexpected new friend on his unexpected journey.

But Lionel had noticed Gulliver's hesitation and was not satisfied. He thought deeply for a moment, wanting to make his point crystal clear. 'The thing is, young prince,' he eventually said, slowly and deliberately, pausing on each word for emphasis: 'To have a following, you must walk away.'

Unconventional Leadership Lesson #5

To GIVE DIRECTION, YOU MUST STAND IN ONE PLACE

Gulliver knew Lionel was right. He turned to the flock and noticed they were still looking at him and talking animatedly. Every now and then, one of them would point a wingtip at him, make some remark (Gulliver was too far away to hear the words, but he could guess what they were saying) and the huddle of geese would all nod or shake their heads with incredulity. Gulliver gave them one last long, indignant stare, turned his back and flew away.

He decided to keep flying south west. He didn't know why, but he felt his adventure was far from over. Also, there was something about the scent of the breeze and the shimmer of the air and the angle of the shadows on the ground . . . Something, but what? There was no logic to flying south west, but it felt right. Besides, the impertinent flock would probably fly south, and the sooner he could get away from them, the . . .

'HONK!'

Gulliver nearly fell out of the sky (again). He recovered from his mid-air half-stall and glanced behind him.

'Honk!'

He couldn't believe . . .

'Honk! Honk! Honk!'

. . . his eyes. There was not one goose, but . . .

'Honk! Honk! Honk! Honk! Honk! Honk!'

. . . the whole flock of geese, all flying in perfect V-formation behind him. And all honking loudly. At first, Gulliver thought they had come to seek their revenge. At any moment, they were surely going to attack him. Then, when they didn't, he thought it must be a nasty trick. Perhaps they were just making fun of him; a parody of follow-the-joke-leader. But strangely, when he looked behind him again, nobody seemed to be laughing. If anything, he thought he detected . . . he must be wrong, but he thought he detected a hint of *respect* in their eyes and an unmistakeable tone of encouragement in their honks.

Gulliver looked straight ahead and continued flying. His head was swimming. What just happened? Was he really leading this flock? The very flock which only moments earlier had been ridiculing and rejecting him? Then he heard the words of Lionel drifting through the mist of his confusion: 'To have a following, you must walk away.' Well, he'd certainly done that. Technically, he'd *flown* rather than *walked* away, but he guessed it amounted to the same thing. Still, that didn't explain the flock's change of heart. Then Gulliver heard the whispers floating on the breeze.

'He must be *the one.*'

'Did you see how he faced that savage beast? Such bravery!'

Gulliver started to smile. 'No, no, no,' he thought. 'You've got it all wrong.' But the windswept chatter continued.

'Our ancient Ganskrit texts *do* foretell of one such as *him*.'

'That's true. And did you notice how he stands out from the crowd, almost without even trying? Such a natural leader!'

Gulliver's mind was reeling. What were they on about? Ganskrit texts? One such as him? What did it all mean? The talk on the breeze was bubbling now.

'The sacred writings *do* speak of an intimate stranger who will lead us on a new path of the wind.'

'You're right. And did you see how confidently he looked at us, before he turned and flew away? He was challenging us; silently commanding us to follow.'

Gulliver couldn't believe what he was hearing. He had to set the record straight. And fast – this was getting out of hand (or was it out of wing?). He was no leader, let alone the 'chosen one'. He was sure it was all just a big misunderstanding. He would explain where he came from, how he got here, and they could go their separate ways – hopefully, as new friends.

Gulliver peeled off from the head of the flock and joined the tail-end of the V. But as he did, he noticed that the geese at the back suddenly went self-consciously quiet. He had just caught the last few words of what they were saying: 'A *messiah*? Pffft! More like a *mis-leader*! That's what he is.' Gulliver had detected a distinct note of hostility in their tone. This new revelation banished any thoughts of having an honest, open dialogue with the geese at the back. Instead, they flew on in silence, each lost in their own very different clouds of thought.

After a few hours of flying in strained silence, marked only by the rhythmic beat of wings and the occasional honk from further up the line, Gulliver couldn't stand it anymore. He *had* to come clean. For better or for worse, he had to face the flock and tell his story. With fresh resolve, he worked his way back up to the front – noticing, as he did, that the honks grew louder and more supportive the closer he got to poll position. As soon as he was back at the head of the flock, he cast about for a place to land.

Soon, Gulliver spotted a watering hole in the distance, which seemed a good choice. He honked – loudly and for the first time – and began to descend. The flock followed. There was a great spectacle of skiing and splashing as they all landed one after another, scattering a nervous herd of antelope from the water's edge. He could sense the flock's relief – they were all tired and the break was welcome. But he also felt a ripple of expectation among them, as they slowly gathered in a horseshoe shape, several layers deep, around him.

The silence inflated like a balloon, as did the pressure Gulliver felt. Around two hundred expectant eyes were trained, unblinking, on him. Most were not unfriendly. If anything, they were filled with a kind of dreaminess; an expression of awe. He knew if he didn't prick the bubble soon, it would burst of its own accord, and he would lose his chance to be heard. But he had been wracking his tiny brain for something profound to say and all he got was the echo of his mother's words: 'Just be nice, Gulliver. Things turn out for the best in the end if you begin by just being nice.' It wasn't the icebreaker he'd hoped for, but it was all he had.

'Hello. My name is Gulliver and I am very pleased to meet you all.'

It was as if he had opened a sluice gate. Pandemonium ensued. There was a cacophony of cheering honks, a frenzied flapping of wings and a tide of garbled questions all being fired at once. Gulliver was astounded. Maybe this leadership lark wasn't so difficult (or so onerous) after all! He raised a wing and a reverent hush descended over the flock.

'Thank you. I don't really know what to say, except that it's so nice to be among fellow geese again. You see, I've been flying solo for what seems like an age.'

There were 'ooos' and 'ahhhs' from the flock.

'The truth is: I was lost. Or at least, I thought I was. But then I met some fabulous friends and it turns out that actually I'm found. You see, Cuthbert (he's a crazy camel with big lips) told me that to find your path you must lose your way and Daphne and Dodger (they're just the sweetest dugongs you ever could meet) made me realise that you must follow yourself and Roodie (he's a nearly-blind mole-rat from Ethiopia) said that to have a vision you must close your eyes and . . . '

Gulliver noticed puzzled looks moving over the flock like the shadow of a cloud passing in front of the sun. He was losing them, he could tell. So, he paused, took a deep breath, and tried again.

'I come from a land far in the north. My flock has its winter home in a place called Scoraig, in Scotland. We are barnacle geese and that is why I look a little different to you. Your flock, from what I understand, is from Egypt (which I visited by the way – a beautiful country, albeit a bit dry for my liking). But anyway, I guess that makes you Egyptian geese. I must admit I find you all very beautiful, with the sheen of your colourful feathers gleaming in the sunlight.'

There were nods of dawning comprehension and titters of flattered agreement. Gulliver continued.

'My flock, and other flocks of barnacle geese, normally fly north in the summer and south in the winter. So why, you might ask, am I flying south in the summer? Well, let's just say that I am having an adventure. I've never been to Africa before and it would be just wonderful if you could join me on my journey of discovery. Not only is there so much to learn and so many new friends to make, but I'm heading for a land so bountiful that you couldn't dream it any better.'

The last bit was made up, of course, which made Gulliver feel a twinge of guilt, but he was remembering what Roodie had said about the Holy Tuber. And anyway, who's to say he was wrong? Maybe such a paradise did exist. And how could they ever know for sure unless they went looking for it in the first place? Even so, Gulliver didn't want a single goose to feel pushed or manipulated into joining his quest. He decided to finish his little speech with an open-ended invitation.

'I realise this is all rather sudden and unexpected and unknown, so I'm going to head off to that small clump of trees over there, beyond the shore, and leave you to discuss the options among yourselves. If you decide to join me, great! Wonderful, in fact. But if you don't, well, I fully understand and it's been lovely to meet you all.'

With a twirling flourish, Gulliver turned away from the flock (not for the first time, he noted) and paddled his way to the far shore, then waddled up the bank and towards the copse of thorn trees. He tried to look as dignified and unhurried as possible, because he knew they were still watching him, but it was a great relief when he finally reached the shade and could hide among the bushveld scrub.

Peering back from behind the tangle of branches and leaves, Gulliver observed the flock. There was a great deal of articulating and gesticulating. He noticed one group, led (if his eyes and memory served him correctly) by the goose he had nearly crashed into. They seemed to be arguing vehemently and loudly *against* joining Gulliver. There was also a pro-joining group led by a rather handsome goose – coincidently the one that had remarked on Gulliver 'looking backwards while flying forwards.' The majority of the flock were milling around, listening and whispering among themselves, but not committing to either one side or the other.

As Gulliver was watching this surreal spectacle, his reverie – and the grand debate on the water – was shattered by a loud CRACK! Panic swept through the group like an icy wind. Another CRACK and nervousness collapsed into chaos. In an almighty confusion of honks and feathers, geese were flying and paddling in all directions, crashing and bumping into one another, going in circles and generally losing their feathery heads.

Gulliver, like many in the flock, knew that shattering sound all too well. It was the 'crack' of a gun being fired and for geese that meant only one thing – extreme danger! Gulliver felt his little heart pounding, but managed to control the rising wave of panic. He looked up, as if he might discover solace in the sky, and to his great surprise, he found instead a kindly face looking down on him. Gulliver let out a startled, muted, honk.

'Shhh!' said the strange face. 'Keep quiet and don't move.'

Gulliver kept quiet and didn't move, but more out of instinct than obedience. He studied the strange face. For one thing, it was a long, long way up in the air. In a weird sort of way, it reminded him of Cuthbert – the same angular snout, big eyes and long eyelashes – except that it also had funny tufted knobs on its head, which in turn was tilted at the end of an unbelievable long neck. In fact, it was the tallest creature Gulliver had ever seen.

'I'm Gillian,' said the creature quietly. 'But my friends just call me Gilly. And those, my friend,' she said, swinging her head in the direction from where the shots had come. 'Those are hunters.'

'Hello Gilly,' whispered Gulliver, a little jittery. 'I'm Gulliver and I'm pleased to meet you, although the circumstances could not have been worse. I know what hunters are, and for that very reason, I must leave right away and help my flock to fly away.' Interesting, Gulliver noted fleetingly, how quickly they had become 'my' flock. Gilly, meanwhile, was shaking her distant head.

'No! Absolutely not. You must not flee. For one thing, the hunters are stalking lions, not birds.' Gulliver felt a fist tighten on his heart, as he thought of Lionel, although of course his friend was many miles away. Gilly continued, 'For another, hunters, like all carnivores, tend to chase whatever runs – or in your case, whatever flies. The best thing you and your flock can do is remain still.'

Gulliver stole a worried glance back at the flock and observed that they were being anything but still. A pang of anxiety clawed up into his throat. Gilly seemed to detect his concern and said reassuringly, 'Don't worry, they are still far away. Why don't you come up here and take a look for yourself. You can sit on my head for a better view.' Gulliver hesitated, but Gilly persisted. 'I really don't mind. In fact, I'd enjoy the company.'

And that is how, in a scene stranger than fiction, Gulliver found himself perched on top of the head of a giraffe in Uganda. It was true what Gilly had said. From up here, he could see the hunting party a long way in the distance, and heading in a direction that posed no threat to them.

'Look! It's Gulliver!'

The exclamation came from one of the geese in the middle of the tangled flock on the water. In fact, wasn't it the one who had noticed that Gulliver had been flying with his eyes closed? Gulliver couldn't be sure, but there was no mistaking its dramatic effect. The eyes of the flock turned to stare at him, as he teetered ridiculously upon his lofty animal tower. Unexpectedly, Gulliver observed, the panic mania of the flock seemed to dissipate, as first one, then another, and finally all of the geese, made a goose-line for the shore and waddled up to the cluster of acacias surrounding Gilly and Gulliver.

Gilly raised a questioning eyebrow, with the hint of a smile on her black, hairy lips. 'Good job,' she remarked, with a tone of surprise.

'But I didn't tell them to come,' Gulliver spluttered. 'I'm not showing them the way. I'm not the chosen one. I'm not even really their leader.'

Gilly frowned, shook her head and then laughed gently. 'That's what *you* think. What matters more is what *they* think. And didn't your mother ever tell you: Sometimes, to give direction, you must stand in one place.'

Unconventional Leadership Lesson #6

TO BE AT THE FRONT, YOU MUST STAY BEHIND

Gulliver wondered what he should say, much less what he should do, as a few hundred goose eyes stared up expectantly at him. Suddenly, a flash of clarity illuminated his petite brain. If he was going to be a leader of this or any flock – and he still wasn't convinced about that – he sure as seaweed couldn't do it pretending to be someone else. He had to be himself, and he had to be honest. Leadership – if that's what he was starting to practice – either had to be common sense, or it wasn't his cup of algae.

And so Gulliver introduced the flock to Gilly (who they nevertheless eyed suspiciously, despite her generous rubber-lipped smile) and he told them about the shooters. 'We are in no danger if we wait here, quietly, until the lion-hunters have moved out of the area. Then we can fly on to less hazardous lands.'

The flock seemed happy with this suggestion – although Gulliver had a feeling they would have been happy with *any* suggestion. What the flock liked, it seemed, was certainty – to be told what to do and when and how. Gulliver wasn't sure he wanted to be telling other geese anything, but for now, he was simply relieved that the flock had settled.

'Are we going to the Ocean Lake? We stop there every year,' a young, bright eyed goose asked.

Gulliver's heart sank. He didn't know where they were going, and he certainly didn't know Ocean Lake. He was about to give up the leadership charade when Gilly came to his rescue.

'If you mean Lake Victoria, which is certainly big enough to be an ocean, that is just a few hours south from here. But I recommend that you steer clear. It seems that hunting season has started early this year, and since wildlife gather around the lake, you might find yourselves in danger.'

Only half of Gulliver's brain was paying attention to what Gilly was saying. The other half was staring incredulously at Gilly's insanely long blue-grey tongue, which waggled like a joyful snake as she talked.

'It may be safer,' Gilly continued, swaying her long neck over the flock as she did. 'If you continue flying south-west, until you reach the Virunga Mountains of Rwanda. There is lots of forest cover that you can shelter under.'

The flock looked uneasy. This was taking them even further off their traditional migration path. They looked up at Gulliver, waiting, he realised, for his 'yay' or 'nay' on the matter.

'You're absolutely right,' proclaimed Gulliver. 'Thank you, Miss Gilly. That is a very wise suggestion. We will rest here in the shade until the sun has cooled in the sky, and then we will set off for Virunga.'

The flock relaxed visibly. If their new, albeit eccentric, leader believed that was the way to go, it must be the right way. Gulliver, meanwhile, felt a ripple of excitement course through his veins. These mountains sounded exotic. And what would the forest be like? He flew down from Gilly's head, nestled under a bush and closed his eyes. The flock clustered around him and did the same, except for one knot of geese (the no-joiners group), which settled a short distance away.

A few hours later, Gulliver decided it was time to go. He hadn't managed to sleep much. Adventure fever was still fizzing in his head and his wings were itching to fly. Gilly was now browsing green tree-top shoots a little way off, so he called to her. 'Thank you again, Miss Gilly. We're on our way. It was so lovely to meet you. I will always remember what you said about standing still.'

'Fly safe and travel well,' replied Gilly. 'Just keep a look out for Mount Sabyinyo. The locals call it "Old Man's Teeth" and you'll know why when you see it. It's an extinct volcano and there are plenty of rock pools for the flock to enjoy.'

The flock, which was engaged in pre-flight preening, liked what they heard and began to share a little of Gulliver's excitement. They took off in a staggered sequence, skimming the waterhole for a last sip of water, and quickly arranged into a neat V-formation. Gulliver, at the head of the flock, waved down at Gilly as they wheeled in the sky and headed south-west.

After a few hours of blissful flight, the landscape began to change below them, with flat khaki giving way to hilly green. Gulliver, meanwhile, was rotating the flock, so that they each took turns at the front. As always, the younger geese were thrilled, and honked most loudly when it was their chance to lead. The flock slipped easily into the recycling rhythm. It was something they had always done, although they didn't really know why. Most assumed it was to keep from getting bored or falling asleep on the wing.

Gulliver, however, knew different. He had once asked his father why the leader of the flock didn't stay at the front. 'You can lead from anywhere in the flock,' his father had replied. 'Even from behind.' He paused and then added, 'But that's not the real reason.'

'What *is* the real reason?' pressed the ever-curious young Gulliver.

'Efficiency,' said his father matter-of-factly.

'What's that?' asked Gulliver.

'It's when you get the most propulsion from the least effort.' Gilgamesh always was a bit of a technical boffin. Gulliver still looked nonplussed, so he continued. 'The lead goose has to work the hardest, right?'

Gulliver nodded. *That* much he knew.

'So, if you rotate the leader, everyone has a chance to regain their strength before working their way back up the V and taking their turn at the front again.'

Gulliver thought he understood. But he was at an age when every answer begged another question. 'But why do we fly in a V, Daddy?'

His father seemed pleased at the question. 'Same reason. That's also for efficiency, son. When we fly in a V, the air passing over each goose's wings gives lift to the geese flying behind, so they don't have to work as hard.'

Gulliver had been satisfied with his father's explanation back then. Now, however, he thought that efficiency was only part of the answer. Rotating leaders and flying in a V was also important because it built camaraderie. It meant every goose felt valued and trusted. It also meant that every goose could not only see where they were going, but also had easy sight of those ahead and those behind. It made them feel like they belonged. They could honk encouragement or exchange gossip. Most importantly, no goose ever felt alone when they were flying in V-formation.'

The sun was just beginning to set as Gulliver was turning these new insights over in his mind. He felt tranquil and at ease. In the shimmering distance, he saw the silhouette of mountains coming into view. Gulliver worked his way back up to the front so that he could guide them over the final stretch. As they came closer, he noticed the jagged outline of the mountain peaks and recalled Gilly's parting words – the locals call it 'Old Man's Teeth'. Now Gulliver could see why. Their grey shape against the reddening sky was majestic, yet somehow also . . .

CRACK!

A bolt of shock shot through the flock. Gulliver's head spun around as an agonised cry pierced the air and a silhouetted goose, feathers fluttering wildly, fell in an arc towards the darkening earth below.

Gulliver didn't have time to think, so he acted on impulse – dropping out of formation like a stone and shouting back to the disappearing flock, 'Keep going! Fly hard and fast! Towards the teeth! Find a safe spot and wait there! I'll catch up with you later!'

Then Gulliver tucked his wings alongside his body and dived towards the flailing, cartwheeling figure that was plummeting to her death. He caught up just in time to knock the goose sideways and get slightly underneath her, cushioning the impact as they both tumbled to the ground and sprawled across the spongy surface of a marshland grove.

Gulliver was slightly stunned, but not badly hurt. He recovered his senses and looked around in a panic for the maimed goose. She was a few metres away. Her eyes were closed and she was not moving. He rushed to her side and felt a flood of relief when he saw her silky beige breast heaving. Moreover, there was no bloodstain on her downy chest, although one of her wings was badly twisted and covered in gore.

'You're going to be alright,' Gulliver whispered, with a calmness and confidence he didn't feel. 'I'm here now, and we're going to get through this together.'

She opened her eyes, glazed and confused. They were deep golden yellow and perfectly set within oval patches of brown. 'Stunningly beautiful,' Gulliver thought, mesmerized. A prickling sensation coursed up his spine and effervesced at the back of his brain. He shook himself back to reality and the emergency situation.

'Where am I? What happened?' she whispered in a choked voice.

'You've been shot – not too badly, I don't think. We're a few miles from our destination in the mountains. But for now, we've got to get you safe and take care of that wound. I'm going to look after you, so don't you worry. What is your name?'

Her eyes seemed to clear and the tension in her body eased slightly. 'I'm Gwendoline, but my friends just call me Gwen.'

'Well, Gwen, I'm Gulliver and . . .'

'I know,' she said dreamily.

'. . . and I'm going to . . .'

'Psst!' The sharp hiss came from some distance away, piercing the murky grey shadows. Gulliver jumped, looking around frantically, trying to pinpoint the source of danger, but seeing nothing. It was getting dark and he was in shock. Maybe his mind was playing tricks . . .

'Psst! Up here!' Gulliver shot a glance skyward and saw, gleaming in the dusky moonlight, two enormous orange eyes. His heart leaped in his chest and he thought, 'This must be the most short-lived rescue attempt in gander history.' Still staring at the saucer-like eyes, Gulliver imagined that the creature in the tree must be enormous. It was probably licking its slavering lips right now and . . .

'We've got to get you and your injured friend out of harm's way,' the spooky eyes said. 'I can hear the hunters' dogs tracking this way. If we work together, we can probably just about manage to help her up this tree and out of sight.' The eyes were moving down the tree trunk now and across the ground towards the two petrified geese.

Gulliver wondered for a split second if he would be delicious or disappointing as dinner. Then, as the creature came closer, he noticed that it was not a monstrous beast at all. In fact, it was a tiny thing – maybe half the size of a goose – and it was . . . Gulliver couldn't find a suitable word to describe it, so he settled on 'very strange.' Its little pointy face was white around the eyes and down its cheeks, but with a tawny furred forehead and snout, so that it looked like a pale heart shape inside a rusty-brown teardrop. The face itself was dwarfed by two enormous outstretched ears, like gigantic antennae. Gulliver also noticed a curling, bushy tail and long, protruding, spidery fingers, which were now reaching out to gently nudge Gwen towards the base of the tree.

Gulliver unfroze and moved in to help. Getting Gwen up the tree was an awkward and painful tango of pushing and pulling, in the midst of wincing and whispered assurances. But eventually, they all made it up into the crown of the forest, safely beyond prying eyes and snuffling noses.

'Thank you.' Gulliver huffed, still out of breath. 'I'm Gulliver. And this. Is Gwen. Very kind. Of you.'

'Don't mention it,' squeaked the little creature. 'My name is Bushy and over there' – another set of orange eyes, smaller but no less bright, appeared suddenly from behind the branches – 'say hello to Baby. We are Galagos, but the jungle folk just call us bush-babies. Now let's take a look at that nasty wound.'

As Bushy treated Gwen's wing – using her dextrous fingers to prepare a special berry paste as disinfectant, then weaving together leaves as a patch and knotting a liana into place as a sling – Baby looked on, inquisitive and wide-eyed, while Gulliver told them of his adventures, ending with how he had abandoned the flock when Gwen was shot.

'Some leader, right?' Gulliver mused, forlorn. 'Abandoning his flock at the first sign of trouble.' He sighed, lowered his head and fell silent, feeling disheartened and unworthy.

Bushy's glowing eyes looked deeply into Gulliver's, full of compassion and empathy. 'But don't you know, my dear,' she said soothingly, reaching out a bulbous finger to wipe away a tear that had slid down Gulliver's cheek. 'Sometimes, to be a leader, you must be the one who stays behind. Even Baby knows that's true.'

Gulliver smiled weakly, unable to conceal the doubt scrawled across his furrowed, feathery brow.

'Ask her,' Bushy persisted. 'Ask Baby how she knows it's true. She's dying to tell you anyway.'

Unconventional Leadership Lesson #7

TO MOVE FORWARD, YOU MUST GO ROUND IN CIRCLES

Baby began chattering away, unravelling a complicated story about how, when he was younger, he was at school one day, and he was on a beetle treasure hunt, and he was with the whole class of eight, but he was winning, along with his best mate, Scratch, and then suddenly their teacher sounded the danger alarm, because she was in the closest tree watching them, and they were about to all run to the tree, like they'd been taught to do and like they had practiced a zillion times, but then he saw a giant African python in the lower branches of that tree, and he thought that's why his teacher had sounded the alarm, but when he checked she was pointing at the sky, and when he looked up he saw an eagle circling, so he knew no one else had seen the snake.

Finally, Baby took a breath. Gulliver and Gwen had been so wrapped up in the story that they had forgotten to breathe as well. Now, they took a gulp of air, just in time to hear Baby gibbering on: 'So I shouted at my class mates to run to the furthest tree, on the opposite side of where we were playing, because there was a snake in the closest tree, and then I ran into the middle of the clearing, and I waved my arms so the eagle would see me and not my friends, and I looked up and saw my teacher screeching for me to run, but she didn't know about the snake, and I waited until my friends reached the faraway tree, and then ran to the bottom of my teacher's tree, and I waved my arms at the snake until it started coming down the trunk to catch me, and then the teacher saw the snake and she went crazy, but it was okay because, by the time the snake reached the bottom of the tree, I had already run across to the other tree, and I was safe and all my class mates were safe and my teacher was safe too.'

Gulliver couldn't tell if Baby was shaking with the excitement of retelling the story, or re-living the fear of his dangerous adventure. Gwen was staring open-beaked in awe at the bravery of this strange, furry little creature, having almost entirely forgotten her own trauma and pain.

'So you see,' concluded Bushy with a wise look in her luminous eyes. 'Sometimes, to be at the front, you must stay behind.' She stroked Baby gently and Gulliver nodded. Maybe staying with Gwen had not been an act of weakness after all.

It took a week before Gwen's wing had healed well enough for her to fly again. During those long, anxious days of waiting, Gulliver gained many more fascinating insights from his warm-hearted hosts. He was amazed that when they were hunting for juicy insects, which was mostly at night, they could cover huge distances by leaping from branch to branch, using the power of their long tails for leverage and balance. He was also comforted, despite worrying constantly about the flock, by the bush-babies' incessant banter, which seemed to encompass a whole symphony of sounds from crying, croaking and chattering, to clucking, cooing and even whistling.

Finally, the day came to leave and Gulliver and Gwen honked goodbye to their new friends, flying at sunrise towards the craggy silhouette of the 'Old Man's Teeth' mountains. The flock was not hard to find – they had landed on the very first large rock pool in their flight path, and had remained there, huddled together, nervously waiting and constantly watching the skies. When Gulliver and Gwen glided in silently and ski-landed nearby, the flock erupted into honking applause, a cacophony of expelled relief and excited curiosity. Gwen's friends fussed around her, while Gulliver told them about the kindness of Bushy and Baby.

Despite their relief at having their leader and injured friend back, however, Gulliver could sense that the flock was restless and ready to move on, so he wasted little time in getting them back on the wing, still flying south-west. As they flew over the jagged mountains and patchwork of forests, Gulliver could see that, under different circumstances, this might have been a perfect resting place. But right now, his priority was the safety of the flock.

After a few hours, the landscape gradually began to flatten out into vast open plains, mottled with acacia trees that cast spotted shadows on the green expanse. Behind him, Gulliver heard excited chattering, as a chain-message was being passed from goose to goose. Finally, it reached him. 'The Great Migration has started!' announced Jack, the goose behind him, as if this was breaking news. Gulliver smiled to himself – apparently, the flock had renamed their adventure 'The *Great* Migration.' He was just about congratulate whoever had come up with the name – a fine idea as a morale booster, he had to admit – when he noticed that Jack and all the geese behind him were staring down in the same direction.

Gulliver followed their gaze and, for a moment, he thought that fatigue must be playing tricks on his sight. It was hard to see clearly, since they were flying so high, but it looked for all the world like a whole forest of dark-coloured trees were moving slowly across the plain. He shut his eyes, shook his head, re-opened them and looked again. The forest was still in motion, rippling and flowing as if a strong wind was moving through the treetops. As he looked more carefully, he decided the moving mass was too dark to be a forest (and anyway, all the forests he had ever seen stood still!). Besides, the movement reminded him of something . . .

Suddenly, it came to Gulliver – ants! The advancing wave far below reminded him of an army of ants. When he was young, he and his friends had often played a game of 'follow-the-ant-trail.' Except this time, they would have to be giant ants, and surely that was taking a small step beyond possibility and a giant leap into improbability.

Just then, Gulliver noticed that Jack was looking expectantly at him, as if waiting for him to say something meaningful. But what? Silently a little cog turned and clicked in his brain and he realised in an instant that The Great Migration was nothing to do with a new name for the flock. It was describing what was happening on the plains below.

As the blood of revelation rushed to his head, Gulliver nodded and blurted out, 'I see! The Great Migration! It's incredible! But what on earth *are* they?' The watching goose's eyes widened in surprise and Gulliver suddenly felt very foolish. How could he be a leader when he was so ignorant? Leaders are meant to know everything about everything. They are meant to be models of cleverness – not some hapless ignoramus from Scoraig. He should have lied and pretended to know. Or better still, he should have kept his beak shut. Instead, now he looked weak and stupid.

Yet, strangely, he saw no disrespect or loss of trust in Jack's eyes. If anything, Jack seemed pleased to have a chance to share something with Gulliver that he didn't already know. 'They are wildebeest,' he said. 'Every year, they migrate, like us. Except *they* do it in their tens of thousands. Pretty amazing, huh?' Gulliver nodded, turned his head and passed on the news to the next goose in the line: 'The wildebeest flock are on their incredible migration.' He pointed knowingly below him.

As they flew on, they saw other strange creatures in flocks on the ground, and each time, Gulliver turned to Jack and asked, 'What flock are those then?' And each time, Jack had the answer. 'That's a *herd* of zebras.' And 'that there is a *herd* of impala.' After the second time, Gulliver spotted what Jack was doing and felt foolish again. But the next time he saw some unfamiliar gathering of animals far below them, he asked Jack, 'What herd is that?' He noticed the faintest trace of a smile in Jack's eyes when he answered, 'Those are elephants.'

Soon, Gulliver caught the familiar scent of brine on the breeze and felt a little reassured. At least he was getting back to familiar territory. Ask him anything about the sea and he was quiz-champion. As if to reassure himself, he honked ahead, 'Ocean ahead, start the descent!' And sure enough, twenty minutes later, a welcome layer of blue appeared below the horizon, growing wider by the minute.

When the grey-blue expanse was just a hundred metres below them, Gulliver circled with the flock and prepared to land. On their final approach, he glimpsed a fin breaching above the surface, and then another. This time, it was Jack's turn to honk to him, 'What strange herd is this?' Gulliver chuckled to himself. 'That, clever Jack, is a school of dolphins.' Jack laughed and replied, 'They look so happy!' It was true. On the rare occasions when he had encountered dolphins in Scoraig, they always seemed to be celebrating the joys of life. So much so that they made him feel happy too.

It was with this thought in mind – once the flock had landed safely and settled into pruning and scavenging for titbits of food - that Gulliver headed off on his own to see if he could find the dolphins. It didn't take long before he spotted the rise and fall of their arched backs in the distance. But just as he was about to fly down and introduce himself, he noticed that the school was no longer cavorting randomly. They had formed themselves into a circle.

Gulliver had not seen the Scoraig dolphins behave like this, so he watched intently to see what they would do next. Suddenly, responding to some inaudible signal, they all dived together, continuing to circle round slowly as they went deeper. Then, again in unison, they started to rise upward, circling faster and faster. Gulliver was amazed at what he was seeing. A shoal of silvery fish was trapped in the middle of the bubbling whirlpool, and they began leaping out of the water in a frenzied panic. As the dolphins breached the surface, they wasted no time in catching their ready-made meal.

Gulliver held back until the feasting had ended and the school returned to their leisurely routine, then he went to meet one particular dolphin who seemed to be the leader. The dolphin greeted him in a spritely voice. 'Hello, feathery friend, my name is Daniel, but my friends call me Danny.' Already, Gulliver was starting to feel better.

'I was just watching your hunting strategy. It was very impressive,' gushed Gulliver.

'Why, thank you!' Danny replied.

'Are you the leader?'

'What makes you think we need a leader?' chortled Danny.

Gulliver hesitated, knocked off balance by the surprising reply. 'Well, now that you ask, I didn't see you giving instructions, and yet it seemed like everyone knew what they were doing.'

'That's because we all have hunting experience. The more experience a team has, the less they need a leader telling them what to do. When we share knowledge, we distribute leadership.' Danny grinned and added, 'We are a *school* after all.'

Gulliver couldn't help but laugh, more from relief than because he thought it was funny. He told Danny about how foolish he had felt earlier when he didn't know about The Great Migration, or that wildlife in Africa gathered in *herds*. And how Jack had been so enthusiastic to share his knowledge.

Danny nodded, seeming happier than ever. 'Being a leader means being prepared to learn and to share learning. The only difference between a leader and a follower is that the leader has had a few more trips around the sun – or around the shoal in our case.'

Danny laughed at his own joke, and his mood was infectious. It was impossible to stay gloomy in his presence. Gulliver was quiet for a few moments, thinking. 'So that means a leader in one situation could be a follower in another!'

Seeing how the revelation lit up Gulliver's face, Danny leapt out of the water. 'Exactly! A leader should never be afraid of not knowing something. Sometimes, we lead the round of learning, and sometimes we allow ourselves to be led, so that next time, we can lead someone else in the circle of knowledge.'

Danny's philosophy sounded so positive, and it made sense too. Gulliver thanked him for cheering him up. 'I was so worried that not knowing something made me look stupid and disqualified me from being a leader. I thought a leader always had to go forward – and it felt like I was going backwards!'

Danny beamed encouragement and, waving a flipper in farewell, saying, 'I think you will find, my fabulous fellow, that you were not going backwards, only entering a new round of knowing. There's a dolphin proverb that says: Often, to move forward, you must go round in circles.'

Unconventional Leadership Lesson #8

TO BE CLEARLY HEARD, YOU MUST BE QUIET

Gulliver returned to the flock and joined in the general milieu of feeding, preening and socialising, but as the sun set, he found himself wondering whether he would have learned such a valuable lesson as Danny's if he had been at Leadership School in London right now. Somehow, he doubted it. All the stories he had heard about the School were of how students were drilled to stand out from the flock; to be brighter and stronger; to fly higher and faster; to honk louder and longer. Gulliver had no conviction that he could be or do any of those things. And yet, here he was, off the coast of Tanzania, apparently the leader of a real flock – and learning how to be a better leader with each passing day.

As the flock slept that night, Gulliver began mulling over his plans to fly south along the coast. He felt comfortable being close to the sea, and by keeping the shoreline in view, he was unlikely to feel quite so lost. As his father would always say, 'Safety first, my boy!' Then again, if he had followed his father's advice, he would never be having this incredible adventure in the first place. But who was he to gamble with the safety of the whole flock, just because he had developed a taste for adventure? On the other hand, the flock seemed to be relishing the discovery of new lands. But . . .

. . . Truth be told, Gulliver was undecided – not a very good thing for a leader to be, he realised. But it was what it was. Then he had an idea. Why not let the flock decide? Admittedly, it was an outlandish idea – not the idea of strong leader at all. But that was the whole point. Anyone in the flock *could* be a leader, if only they were given a chance. Maybe it was someone else's turn. Thinking along these lines made him suddenly feel a whole lot better. As he felt the weight lifting from his wings, he fell promptly and soundly asleep.

The next morning at sunrise, Gulliver gathered the flock. They all seemed very contented, having had time to feed and rest. All eyes were on him, expectant, and so he began to speak. 'I have decided,' he said in his most casual voice. 'I have decided . . . not to make a decision.' Confusion rippled visibly across the faces of the flock, but no one made a sound. 'What I mean to say is, from here on, the journey going forward is entirely up to you.' Confusion turned to frowns of worry. 'In other words, you get to decide where we go next.' Gulliver expected cheers of joy. Instead, there was an involuntary collective gasp and one goose, a youngster called Benjamin, blurted out: 'No way! He's joking, right?'

'Yes way!' rejoined Gulliver. 'You are all intelligent geese. And not only smart, but experienced too. Many of you have migrated down through Africa before, whereas this is my first time. Surely you know better than me which way to fly from here. So, that being the case, I'm listening with all ears. Any and all suggestions are welcome.'

His words were greeted with stunned silence and a vigorous, incredulous shaking of heads and clicking of beaks. Finally, a self-assured goose named Veneta rallied to the call and spoke up. 'Maybe Gulliver's right. We all know our destination is the southern tip of Africa. And we all know that we are now on the east coast, near the exotic island of Zanzibar. Cape Agulhas is probably about 5,000 kilometres away in a south-westerly direction, as the goose flies. So I say we head south-west.'

Gulliver was impressed. Why wasn't *she* the leader? She was knowledgeable, articulate and decisive, all traits he seemed to lack. He would be more than happy to hand things over to her, here and now, and follow her to wherever she said they should go. He was sure the flock would share his glowing sentiments. He was wrong.

First there were whisperings. 'Who is *she*? And what gives *her* the right to tell us where to go?'

Then the whisperings turned into audible grumblings. 'Was she even *on* the last migration? Besides, she looks too young to know anything worth anything.'

Soon, the grumblings had become undisguised, indignant honks of dissent. 'What about the dangers? The coastline is safer. Are you trying to take Gulliver's crown? Remind me, who is your mother and father? Anyway, I bet you haven't even been to leadership school.'

Gulliver thought this whole line of questioning was not only crazy; it was downright unfair. He should remind them that *he* was no one special. And *he* hadn't been to leadership school. And besides, Veneta's proposed action sounded like a well thought-out plan. He was going to say all these things and more, but the squawking and squabbling of the flock drowned out his attempt to be heard.

'We should ask the oldest among us – the venerable Gandalf, who is surely the wisest – which way we should go,' said one particularly vocal goose. A balding Gandalf looked surprised at hearing his name and visibly grew an inch taller. He puffed up his feathers, cleared his throat and … Well, he was going to say that they should consult the time-old map. They must figure out how to get back onto the trusted migration path that he had flown for the past 20 years, and his grandfather had flown for 20 years before that. But someone else was already honking contradictory advice: 'Forget that! The elders can't help us now. We are in new territory. What we need are entrepreneurs. We need our best young scouts to plot a path for us.'

Gulliver watched the spectacle in dismay. He could see that nobody was listening to anybody else. Everyone had an opinion – that much was clear – but they seemed less interested in debating its merits and more interested in proclaiming their views louder than their neighbour. Somehow, unwittingly, Gulliver had turned a peaceful, compliant flock into a cacophonous rabble of rowdy geese. It reminded him of the politicians back home when they debated policies for Scoraig.

The unruly flock's behaviour was disturbing to Gulliver. But he was even more concerned about how the debacle had affected Veneta. She had moved quietly away from the squabbling crowd and was now floating on her own, head lowered, looking shell-shocked. He had only seen that look once before, when his friend Keith had accidentally flown into a glass window and stumbled to his feet afterwards looking stunned and dazed.

Gulliver's first instinct was to scream at the flock – to chastise them for their insensitivity and to castigate them for their stupidity;

to tell them (in words that he wouldn't want his mother to hear) to 'shut their bleedin' beaks for once and for all!' His second impulse was to ignore the flock and to go across to Veneta to offer her whatever words of sympathy and comfort he could muster. Instead, he had a flash of insight, and decided on a third option.

Gulliver had noticed that Veneta was almost directly opposite him, on the other side of the raucous gaggle. Besides this, he intuitively understood that she did not need his sympathy, but rather his support. And so, with head held high and beak tightly closed, Gulliver slowly made his way through the middle of the noisy flock. As he did so, they were forced to clear a channel, so that the sea appeared to part before him. Somehow, this action – and his own silence – acted like a muffling contagion, and one by one, the flock fell silent.

By the time he had made it across to the other side of the flock and was gliding over the gap towards Veneta, all eyes were on him. As he got near, Veneta raised her head hesitantly, with apology in her eyes, as if she was anticipating a rebuke. But Gulliver said nothing. Instead, he eased on past her flank, turned and positioned himself in a stately fashion directly behind her. She turned and looked at him, as comprehension slowly dawned. He nodded imperceptibly, yet remained silent.

Veneta turned back to face the flock, then with an elegance that must have come from many hours of practice, she took off straight over the heads of the flabbergasted geese, with Gulliver right behind her. She circled once and flew a second time over the gobsmacked flock. This time, first one, then another and another, and finally all of the flock took off in the wake of Veneta and Gulliver. Only once every last goose was in formation behind them did Gulliver break the silence with a poignant honk.

The flock echoed the call, but with noticeably less enthusiasm than when Gulliver had led the flock. They were on course again, but the whole affair had left Gulliver with a lot to think about. Why had his invitation to take charge of their own destiny ended up in bickering and chaos? Why had they not supported Veneta's original proposal? Was it because she was a *she*? Or because she was seen as a young upstart? Or was it because they felt insecure without an established leadership figure?

By mid-afternoon, they had arrived at a beautiful lake, which seemed almost as big as the sea. Since Veneta was leading, Gulliver didn't say anything to prompt her, but he was glad when she started to descend and finally brought the flock down to land on an island called Likoma in the middle of the lake. In contrast to the morning's excitement, most of the geese seemed subdued and tired, as if squabbling had sapped them of their usual exuberance. As they settled down for the evening, Gulliver went out on the water to be alone.

At least, he thought he was alone, but then he spotted bubbles rising to the surface nearby. He nearly jumped out of his feathers when the bubbles were replaced first by two round ears and then two eyes and a massive head. After regaining his composure, Gulliver introduced himself and was met by the biggest grin he had ever seen in his life. 'Hello Guvvivvar,' the smiling head replied. 'My name is Haroldopolis the Hippopotamus, but my friends just call me Harold the Hippo, or Harry for short. Would you like to play with us?'

As he said 'us' the water around Gulliver was suddenly frothing with bubbles and two more heads popped up. 'This is my sister, Holly, and my brovver, Hubert. And this, he said to his siblings. 'This is my new fwend Guvvivar.' Gulliver's mood lightened immediately and he said he was happy to meet them and would be delighted to play. But then it turned out the game was to see who could stretch their mouths the widest, and since Gulliver's beak was no match for the impressive jaws of Harry, Holly and Hubert, he offered to be the judge of who had the widest yawn, which was still fun.

They were just about to start a second round of the game (Holly won the first) when another set of ears and eyes appeared a short distance away – much bigger ones this time. No sooner had they surfaced than Gulliver noticed one of the ears rotate, one of the eyes wink and then the head was gone, leaving only a set of ripples behind. Even stranger still, his newfound friends had disappeared as well, submerged without a word of explanation, or even a goodbye.

Gulliver was curious to know what had happened, so he held his breath and ducked his head under the water. He concluded that this was a dream, because it looked for all the world as if his friends were out for a stroll on a sunny day, behind what appeared to be their mother, except that they were walking on the bottom of the lake. Then it turned out he was not dreaming, because the mother slowly and gracefully floated up to the surface and greeted him with an even more enormous smile. 'I am Henrietta, and I believe you have met my children already.' Gulliver said hello and told her about their game and how amazed he was when they suddenly disappeared, without her even having said a word or made a sound.

Henrietta let out a broad toothy chuckle. 'Yes, that is the Hippo way,' she said, rotating her ears (first one then the other) and winking, as if to emphasise the point. 'When you spend a good deal of your days underwater, you quickly learn to give directions using silent signals. In our world, actions speak louder than words. All good mothers know that to be heard clearly, you must be quiet.'

Gulliver nodded, with fresh understanding settling like a gathering mist in the valley. He thanked Henrietta and said goodnight. It was only later, as he was dozing off to sleep that one of the other geese heard him murmuring to himself, 'Not only all good mothers, but all good leaders too.'

Unconventional Leadership Lesson #9

TO EMBRACE THE FUTURE, YOU MUST LET GO OF THE PAST

Gulliver woke to the murmuring of the flock, all of whom were, curiously, standing in a circle around him, pointing and whispering and giggling. He closed his eyes. Perhaps he was still dreaming? But when he opened his eyes again, the flock was still there. Lapping tides of confusion soon turned into angry waves of indignation crashing upon the sleepy shores of his consciousness. He was about to unleash a string of curses that would have made their feathers curl when he noticed a commotion at the back of the flock.

'What's the matter with you? Quit your rubbernecking and clear off! Didn't your mothers teach you any manners? You're acting like a brood of clucking chickens!' The crowd began to disperse, sheepishly.

Gulliver's hot anger melted into a warm, cosy feeling that he could not name. He knew that voice! He felt his whole body perk up, as he shook the remains of sleep from his wingtips. 'Good morning, Gwen,' he said, trying to sound suave, but instead croaking like a frog.

Gwen laughed – a tinkling sound, which echoed the days they had spent together with Bushy and Baby in Rwanda. Gulliver cleared his throat, recovering. 'Your wing looks good as new.'

'It is,' she replied. 'Thanks to you . . . and those cuddly friends we made in the forest. Sometimes I wish we had never re-joined this flock of gossiping hens.'

'Ah, yes, about that . . . ' Gulliver's confusion returned. 'Thanks for disrupting the gawk-fest. But I still don't understand what that was about. Why were they staring and pointing like that?'

Gwen's self-confident tone changed. Quietly, almost apologetically, she said, 'You were . . . er . . . you were talking in your sleep. You said . . . um . . . some strange things.'

Gulliver felt the blood drain from his face. For a few seconds, he couldn't breath. He wished the island would swallow him up. What had he said? Had he confessed his . . . affections . . . for Gwen? He felt so stupid. No one wants to follow a love-sick goose, let alone a nocturnal blabbermouth.

Gwen saw the fright in his eyes and reassured him. 'It was nothing terrible. Nothing embarrassing. Just strange. Enigmatic.'

Gulliver got a grip on himself. Maybe he could still salvage his pride and quietly disappear. But first, he had to know. 'What did I say, Gwen? Please, be honest. Word-for-word.'

Gwen hesitated. 'It didn't make any sense really. You just kept going on about ducks. 'Brace of ducks. Not good enough. Flush of ducks. To fall short is to fail. Paddling of ducks. Missing the mark. Raft of ducks.' The flock is wondering what it means . . . the ducks."

Gulliver hardly heard Gwen. As soon as she had said 'ducks' he was back in his nightmare. It was a recurring dream that haunted Gulliver. The worst part was, it was also true. He was doubly embarrassed. How could he tell them? They would lose all respect for him. They would not believe him capable of being a leader. And rightly so.

Gwen was looking at him intently. There was compassion in her eyes. The eyes of the flock were still on him too, although they pretended not to look. Curiosity filled their glances. Yet he could not face them. Not now. They could not know the depths of his shame. Some secrets are meant to stay hidden.

Gulliver murmured an apology to Gwen, got up and glared defiantly at the flock. Brusquely, he honked, 'Gwen will lead the flock today!' It was not a question, or an invitation. It was a statement. He gazed around, daring anyone to challenge him. He searched their beady little eyes for defiance, or even hesitation. He was in the mood for a fight. But no one questioned him. They almost seemed relieved to be moving on. Pre-flight preening began in earnest.

That day, Gwen maintained their south-westerly course. The flock seemed to have forgotten the morning's incident. But Gulliver had not. And neither had Gwen. Each time she rotated past him, she gave him a strange look, as if he had betrayed her. He felt bad, but how could he tell her, let alone the flock, about his Big Failure? It would expose him as a charlatan leader. She would see how dishonest he'd been by accepting leadership of the flock.

As the flock's wings beat hypnotically, his mind drifted back to that dark day, which he could never forget, no matter how hard he tried. It was his seventh Eggday and the flock of Scoraig had gathered for the customary celebrations. He and his friends were showing off their flying tricks over the bay, while the adults gossiped on the shore. Everyone seemed happy. Until the scream. That scream still echoed in his nightmares.

One of the parents was shrieking and pointing to a freshwater rock pool, just inland. Gulliver saw a gosling flapping in distress. He dived to see what all the commotion was about. The youngster, who he recognised as Little Sean, seemed to be caught in something. Perhaps it was a fisherman's net? He landed close by and, to his horror, saw that a snapping turtle had grasped Little Sean by the wing and was dragging him under.

Gulliver launched himself at the turtle, pecking furiously. Momentarily distracted, the turtle loosed his grip on Little Sean and turned on Gulliver. Quick as a flash, the turtle had Gulliver's neck between his sharp, bony jaws, and was biting down hard. Pain shot through Gulliver's body. Adrenaline flashed in his veins. The next instant, he was yanking his head back, manically beating his wings and kicking his legs wildly. At last, his neck wrenched free and Gulliver made his escape, thrashing and splashing as he cleared first the water and then the rocks.

His heart thundered in his ears. His neck pulsed with pain. Blood trickled from the wound. And his mind screamed, over and over: 'Danger! Away! Escape!'

Gulliver flew – faster and harder and further than ever before in his life. He did not look back. Fear chased him like a rabid hound. He was in a race for his life. If he hesitated, he was lost. If he turned around, he was doomed. If he stopped, he would surely die.

By the time Gulliver calmed down enough to think clearly, he was miles from the shore, miles from the rocky pool, miles from . . . Oh no! Little Sean! What became of Little Sean? He had to save him!

Gulliver wheeled in the sky, but he already knew it was too late. He had abandoned the gosling, who stood no chance against the snapping jaws of that terrible turtle. Gulliver felt the strength drain from his wings. He slowed, then stopped, crash-landing on a barren hilltop. The sun went behind dark clouds – and Gulliver wept.

That night, he hid beneath a thorny gorse bush and cried himself to sleep. Everything was a blur after that. Time stood still and Gulliver never noticed whether it was day or night. Later they told him that it was four days before the search party from the flock found him – hungry, bedraggled and ashamed, still hidden under the bush.

'Are you alright?' It was Gwen, flying beside him, her voice gentle and tender. Gulliver jerked out of his reverie and found, to his further embarrassment, that he had been crying. He could not find the words to speak, so he simply nodded.

Gwen made her way back to the front of the V and announced their descent to find a resting place for the night. As they landed near a clump of acacia trees, Gulliver could hardly believe that the sun was already low in the sky. They must have been flying all day. Even the terrain was different – dry, scrubland savannah.

Gulliver found Gwen and thanked her for her concern earlier. Then, to change the topic, he quickly added, 'We will need to find water. It looks like there may be a small pool across the way, near those gigantic boulders. I will check that it's safe.'

Before she could reply, he turned and headed in the direction of the blurry granite stones. But as he came closer, to his great surprise, the boulders began to move. Gulliver stifled an undignified squawk and continued, more slowly now, towards the pool. He felt himself trembling. In fact, the ground itself seemed to be shaking. Was this what an earthquake felt like? He had heard about them in the gosling scare-stories his grandmother had told him. Gulliver was scared, but he couldn't turn back – the flock was probably watching. So, he pretended he was brave.

Then a deep rumbling sound came from the strange, moving boulders . . . and Gulliver could swear it seemed to be saying 'Heeelloooooo brrrraaaavvve ffffrieeeennnnd.' Was he still dreaming? He shook himself and looked again. The giant stones seemed to have faces. Weird faces – massive ears like some flat jellyfish, a long nose like kelp seaweed and twinkling eyes amidst the wrinkliest crinkliest skin he had ever seen.

Gulliver knew he was a coward, but he was not rude, and so he replied. 'Good evening, gentle giant. My name is Gulliver, of the feathered clan of Scoraig, many, many leagues north of here . . . although I'm not sure where *here* is exactly.'

One of the kind, grey faces smiled, producing yet more wrinkles, as impossible as that seemed. 'Welcome, Gulliver, to the land of Zimbabwe, the House of Stones. My name is Edgar and this is my elephant family. Why so sad?'

For some reason, Gulliver felt totally safe among these curiously wonderful leviathans. Sometimes, it seemed, it was easier to trust strangers than friends, especially when they had such enormous, understanding eyes. Gulliver told Edgar about the embarrassing events of the day, including the recurring nightmare and his seventh Eggday shame.

Edgar bowed his head empathetically. 'Little Sean may have lost his struggle for life, but it seems you both battled valiantly, against the odds?'

Gulliver swallowed hard and blinked back more tears, shaking his head. 'No, Little Sean did not die. He was rescued by my father, the great and brave Gilgamesh.'

Edgar smiled slowly. 'That is good. Your father was looking out for you – and the rest of the flock.'

Gulliver shook his head again, dejected. 'But I should have saved Little Sean. Instead, I flew away, as only a coward would. When they found me and I returned to the flock, my father spoke only once about my shame. "Gulliver," he said. "Always remember that you are a goose. Ducks flee in the face of danger. Geese stay and fight. You fell short of the mark. But you are still young. One day, you will show your true colours." That is all he said. He never spoke of it again.'

A tear rolled down Gulliver's cheek and Edgar wiped it away gently with the tip of his long nose. 'Let me tell you a story. Do you know how the elephant got its trunk?'

'It's trunk?' replied Gulliver, bemused.

'Yes, this long, rubbery nose of ours.' Edgar smiled and patted Gulliver playfully on the head. 'Once upon a time, we all had short noses, like all the other animals. But one young elephant – Edison was his name – was curious about what crocodiles ate for dinner. So he went to the river and asked a cunning crocodile named Caesar. "Come closer," smiled the toothy Caesar. "I will whisper the answer in your ear." Foolish little Eddie leaned closer and Caesar grabbed his nose between his sharp teeth and began pulling him into the river.'

'Well,' continued Edgar, 'young Eddie was so shocked and frightened – and mad at having been tricked by Caesar – that he pulled as hard as he could. So hard, in fact, that his nose began to stretch. The pain was terrible, but still he did not stop pulling – until finally Caesar gave up and let go.'

'At first,' rumbled on Edgar, 'young Eddie felt ashamed and hid from the herd. He had been so foolish – and now he looked ridiculous with his long nose. But then a strange thing happened. He discovered that having a long nose was quite useful. He didn't have to bend to pick up branches and he could give himself a shower. As he demonstrated his new skills, all the other elephants became jealous. And so, one by one, they went to the river and asked Caesar what he ate for dinner. And one by one, they came back with stretched noses.'

Gulliver was so fascinated by the story that he almost forgot his own shame. Edgar finished by asking, 'What do you think the moral of the story is, brave Gulliver?'

'Well,' mused Gulliver. 'I suppose that what seemed like a disaster for Eddie, turned out to be a blessing in disguise.'

'Precisely true,' nodded Edgar. 'In fact, Edison ended up being a great leader. But not before he accepted his mistakes and moved on. What would have happened if Eddie had stayed hidden away, unable to overcome his shame?'

Gulliver knew this was a rhetorical question. And as his wise friend looked down on him with caring eyes, Gulliver started to see his childhood trauma in a different light. Perhaps failure did not disqualify him as a leader? Maybe falling short was not the end, but the beginning of leadership?

With comprehension dawning like the promise of sunrise, Gulliver mused aloud. 'It's almost as if . . . to embrace the future, a leader must first let go of the past.'

Edgar let out a startling trumpet of delight. 'Just so, brave Gulliver. Just so.'

Unconventional Leadership Lesson #10

TO FIND THE SHOOTS, YOU MUST KNOW YOUR ROOTS

Gulliver thanked Edgar for his advice and returned to address the flock. 'Our new friends, the elegant elephants, tell me that the water in the pool is safe to drink and they will protect us from any harm for as long as we want to rest here. So please, go and drink your fill, take your baths and preen your feathers. When you return, I will tell you a tragic tale with a happy ending – about ducks.'

There was excitement and no small degree of chattering in the flock as they made their way to the pool. The elephants had retreated from the pool and stood like a circle of sentinels, guarding the flock against any unwelcome visitors. As the other geese were faffing and flapping and fluffing in the pool, Gulliver remained a short distance away, with his back to them. He was practicing his speech. 'This is a story about a young goose who was celebrating his seventh EggDay . . . '

Gulliver was so absorbed in his rehearsal that he didn't notice the ominous puce-coloured storm clouds that were building great towers in the sky. Nor did he notice the edgy tone that slowly crept into the gabbling of the flock behind him. He did not even notice the gathering breeze ruffling his feathers, or the first raindrops that landed in little puffs of dust around him.

By the time Gulliver did notice the storm – when one especially heavy raindrop landed right in the middle of his forehead – it was too late. As he turned to face the flock, a violent gust of wind blew him clean off his feet and rolled him like tumbleweed away from the pool. He scrabbled and squawked and flapped, fighting to regain his balance, and taking off in a blur of splattering mud and pelting rain.

No sooner had he lifted from the ground than the gale force wind swept him further away from the flock. He craned his neck and strained his eyes to look back through the curtain of stinging rain, but he could only make out a muddle of white and grey in the distance. Gulliver was battling to stay airborne as the storm tossed and shook and battered him eastwards.

Gulliver's whole mind and body was now focused on survival. If he crashed, he would surely die. One thought consumed his entire being: 'A leader – no matter how good – is no good to anyone if he is dead.' Gulliver flapped and strained and floundered. The wind screeched and howled. The rain pounded and thundered. Lightening cracked and flashed.

Yet in the midst of the chaos and noise, Gulliver thought he heard a deep rumbling voice. Could it be the Great Gander in the Sky, calling him home? Should he give up the struggle and go to that place where the sun always shines and no storms ever disturb the blissful blue sky? But then Gulliver suddenly recognised the voice – it was Edgar's – and he could just make out the words too:

'Hoooollllldddd   oooonnnnttooooo   yooourrseeeeelfffff, brrraaaavvveee Guuullliiiiverrrr . . . '

Gulliver didn't know what the words meant, but they gave him comfort nevertheless. He would fight the storm and win, and then he would return to the flock and guide them safely to the Fairest Cape.

The storm seemed to last a lifetime. Gulliver's wings ached, his heart pounded, his body felt bruised and his face stung. Yet still he stayed aloft, batted and buffeted ever eastward. 'Hold onto yourself, hold onto yourself, hold onto yourself.' The mantra kept him going, gave him strength he never knew he possessed. Slowly, the words started to make sense. When leaders face the storm alone and have nothing left to cling to, they can still hold fast to their beliefs. When leaders are stranded in the wilderness with no resources, they can still draw on their inner strength. When leaders are in the eye of chaos with no direction, they can still steer by the light of their higher purpose.

As Gulliver's mind was meditating thus, his body was being strained to the limit. Below him, through the torrential haze, he saw a blur of brown and green become a blur of turquoise and blue. He had been swept out to sea and soon, no land was in sight. Panic rose like bile in Gulliver's throat, but he fought it down. 'Hold onto yourself. Hold onto yourself.'

Then, just as Gulliver thought that even holding onto himself had become impossible, the wind started to die down and the rain began to ease. The sky of black and grey shadows grew lighter and eventually dispersed. The white froth of waves below him lost their crests and finally collapsed to become an indigo mirror stretched to the horizon.

Gulliver knew he must rest, but he was afraid that if he landed in the middle of the ocean, he would never find his way back. His grandfather, the old and wise Gengis, used to say that even though geese can float, they cannot swim. 'We are not fish, young Gulliver,' he would lecture. 'Geese belong on the land and in the skies. We need to feel the earth beneath our webbed feet to know where we stand. All that endless nothingness of the ocean will rob you of your bearings. You may think the blue is harmless, but before you know it, the ocean can swallow you up.'

'Why?' Gulliver would always ask. 'Because without any landmarks, geese have nothing to strive towards,' Gengis would reply. 'And without a goal, even the most intrepid leader will lose his calling. If we don't know where to go, we don't go anywhere.' On and on his grandfather would talk. Gulliver wasn't sure he believed everything Tata Gengis said, but he wasn't going to take any chances.

Luckily, land soon appeared on the horizon and the closer he came, the wider it stretched before him. Surely it was too big to be an island, Gulliver thought. Had he inadvertently discovered a new continent? Yet almost as soon as this idea appeared, it vanished again. He was too tired to think. The big land, extending a long way south, was intimidating. But Gulliver noticed a smaller island, green and lush, just off the coast. As soon as he reached the forest canopy, he found a small clearing and landed. Within minutes, he was in a deep, dreamless sleep.

Gulliver slept soundly for a day and a night. When he awoke – and even before he opened his eyes – his heart filled with fear. He had not escaped. The storm had returned to claim him. He could hear the high pitched howl of the wind. Gulliver wished he had never woken up. He didn't think he could survive another storm, not even by holding onto himself.

Yet as he listened, eyes still closed, he noticed that the howling was strangely melodic. It was more like a song than the screeching gale had been. What's more, there was an echo, almost as if someone was calling and another was replying. Gulliver's curiosity got the better of him. He opened his eyes.

Above him, the whole world was green. Not one green, but a million greens. The verdant kaleidoscope soothed his eyes. He took a deep breath and smelled the sweet dank aroma of earth and leaves and decomposing wood. Perhaps heaven was not sunny blue skies, as he had been taught, but leafy green forests. Then again, he wasn't sure there would be giant orange eyes peering down at him in Gander heaven.

The radiant eyes were set in a furry black face, edged with tufts of white. Gulliver did not panic. His heart did not even beat faster. Somehow, he had seen too much – been through too much – to be afraid. In the dark bowels of the storm, he had faced his demons and survived. Gulliver had discovered that a leader's greatest enemy was not someone or something *out there* but fears *in here* – the insecurities within his own mind.

The furry creature, which Gulliver now noticed had a long black and white tail, seemed curious and was climbing down the nearby tree trunk. Gulliver was reminded of Bushy, but this animal was much bigger. It had huge leathery hands, powerful arching haunches and gripping feet that worked perfectly well as a second set of hands.

Gulliver still felt weak, but he was not about to forsake his manners. 'Hello inquisitive friend,' he quacked. 'My name is Gulliver. Please forgive my bedraggled state. I was caught in a storm and blown here from the Land of Stones. I thought I had died, but then I awoke to your beautiful song.'

A smile spread across the creature's small pointy face. 'Hello Gulliver. My name is Lova and the song you heard is the morning forest report of the Indri lemurs. Each family shares the news and weather forecast from their part of the jungle. The cyclone that brought you here was a bad one. It has done a lot of damage to our homes, but no one was hurt. And you will be glad to hear that there are no more storms predicted for the rest of the week.'

Gulliver felt a leaden weight lift from him. He felt safe and immediately welcome among Lova and his forest friends. He had nothing to hide and nothing to lose. 'The truth is, I am lost, again. Even more lost that when I first got lost.' Lova cocked his head to one side, looking puzzled. There was nothing to do but to give an honest account of his adventures. As he did so, Lova listened patiently and the rest of his family gathered around in the nearby branches, nodding and tut-tutting, smiling and shaking their heads, as the tale unfolded.

When Gulliver had finished telling of his journey, Lova opened his long arms wide and said, 'You are most welcome in Nosy Be, our island off the island of Madagascar. The tropical storms bring many refugees to our shore and they are all granted asylum for as long as they want to stay. Many never leave and our wild kingdom is all the more rich for that.'

'That is very kind of you,' replied Gulliver. 'But I need to get back to my flock. They will be worried. And besides, I need to finish what I started. Our great migration is not yet at an end. Also, I don't belong here, in this foreign land, albeit a beautiful paradise.'

'We understand,' said Lova. 'But you are a long way from the mainland of Africa now. You will need to rest and eat and gather your strength for the flight back across the seas. While your body recovers from its great ordeal, tell us more about where you belong. We are always most interested to hear about the lodestar that guides our refugee friends.'

Gulliver wasn't sure what a lodestar was and – now that he had been asked so poignantly – he wasn't sure he knew where he belonged either. 'Maybe I don't belong anywhere,' he replied forlornly.

'Everyone belongs somewhere,' reassured Lova. 'Why don't you tell us about your family and your flock in Scoraig. Knowing where you come from is the first step in finding out where you truly belong.'

And so, under the mesmerising gaze of his lemur friends, Gulliver spoke about his mother Glynnis and his father Gilgamesh, his grandfather Gengis and his grandmother Gwain. He recounted the traditions and folktales of the Scoraig flock – the daring escapades of their ancestors and the enduring taboos of community life. As he spoke of all this, Gulliver began to feel the tug of his connection to home, the invisible threads that tied him to his family, his friends and his forebears.

'It's strange,' he concluded. 'Scoraig is my home and the flock are my kith and kin. Yet since being away, I am less certain that I belong there.'

Lova smiled a toothy smile and nodded with comprehension. 'For a long time, we lemurs felt the same way. Where we come from is a mystery. Our folktales tell us that there are few like us anywhere else in the world. Yet the monkeys and apes of Africa are our brothers and sisters. In the end, we have learned that where we belong is where we can flourish.'

When Gulliver heard this, it felt like cracks in the shadowy forest canopy of his confusion opening up to let the shafts of clear light shine through. Lova was continuing: 'There are many different kinds of lemurs and each one needs different things to flourish. We love the juicy leaves of these trees,' he said pointing to the branches where his family were still peering down. 'Yet some of my cousins in this very same forest eat bamboo.'

Gulliver could see the logic, but wasn't sure how it applied to him. Still, he continued to listen. 'I am the leader of my family of six,' Lova was saying. 'And it is my job to find places in the forest where we can flourish. The best way for me to lead, however, is not to randomly jump from tree to tree, hoping to get lucky. Rather, I must scout along the forest floor to see where our favourite trees are growing. Do you understand?'

Gulliver hesitated, so Lova carried on. 'A leader must scout for where opportunities are planted, not where they are blowing in the wind. Then we can climb up and enjoy our rewards.'

The light in Gulliver's head was growing brighter now, but Lova wanted to leave him in no doubt about the lesson he was trying to convey. 'What I'm trying to say,' Lova said with deliberate emphasis. 'Is that, for a leader to find the shoots, first he must discover the roots.'

Gulliver finally understood. To know where he belonged, he had to know where he was rooted. But the fruits are not in the same place as the roots. He would always be connected to his history and his family and his Scoraig flock, but the place where he belonged was where he could thrive.

Gulliver thanked Lova for his welcome and his wisdom and set off to explore the island, while he regained his strength. As he wandered on the beaches and drifted on the gentle waves, as he rested under the coconut trees and met new lemur friends in the forest, he thought less about his Scoraig home and more about the flock stranded in Zimbabwe. He hoped they were all safe and unafraid. And more than anything, he prayed that Gwen had come to no harm.

Unconventional Leadership Lesson #11

TO FLY THE HIGHEST, YOU MUST CLIP YOUR WINGS

Gulliver woke to another day in paradise. Yet it was a paradise without those he cared most about. It was a paradise with nothing to strive for. Gulliver had enjoyed the hospitality of the lemurs for more than a week now and he decided that the time had come to leave. His injuries had mended, his strength had returned and his wanderlust grew with each passing day. Gulliver sought out Lova's advice one last time. 'What is the best way to return to Africa, kind friend?'

Lova raised his hand, as if in benediction. 'First, we must thank you for the many gifts you have shared – especially the lessons of your remarkable odyssey.' He spread his arms and continued. 'You will always have a place in our hearts and on our island off the island of the great continent.' Lova pointed to the shore of Madagascar across the bay. 'Your best route is to follow the coast south, until you reach the avenue of sky roots. Rest there overnight. Then fly directly west and – with a wind at your back – you should reach the mountains of Africa before nightfall.'

Gulliver thanked Lova and said goodbye to his dear family. It felt good to be on the wing again. As he hugged the coastline, he passed over many fishing villages with strange shaped boats. Gulliver kept scanning the blue horizon and the white clouds for signs of 'sky roots' but to no avail. Soon the lush green forests were replaced by dry scrubland.

As the sun began to dip down low, Gulliver decided to find shelter for the night and continue his search the next day. In the distance, he saw a clump of weird-looking trees breaking the monotony of the flat land, so he sought refuge among their lengthening shadows. There were also shallow pools nearby, displaying beautiful reflections of the clouds and the trees, with their fat trunks, splayed branches and sparse leaves.

After quenching his thirst, Gulliver gazed at the reflections of the extraordinary trees. Seen upside down, the tangle of frayed branches looked just like . . . Gulliver's tiny brain stopped in its tracks, overwhelmed by its own insight. He took a deep breath and his mind-cogs began whirring again. The branches looked just like *roots*! 'So . . . ' Gulliver pondered aloud. 'These trees must be the sky roots Lova had talked of!' Gulliver looked at the way the trees formed two rows. 'And this must be the avenue of sky roots.'

Gulliver felt a wave of relief wash over him. He was one step closer to re-joining the flock. That night, he slept soundly and dreamed he met a rainbow creature in the branches of the sky trees. The animal was almost like a lizard – but with scaly skin that changed colour, a thin curly tail, a long coiled-up tongue and cone-shaped eyes that moved in different directions. He reminded Gulliver of a wise old man.

'My name is Charles the chameleon,' he whispered in the dream. 'I am here to wish you *bon voyage* from our land of baobabs. Always remember, leaders that survive in the jungle are those that fit their surroundings. Sometimes, it is better for a leader to blend into the background.' Charles changed colour to become indistinguishable from the branch he was clinging to, as if to emphasise the point. 'Leaders that stand out too much are asking to become someone else's lunch.'

Gulliver woke refreshed and was cheered to note that a gentle wind was at his tail as he set off westward across the ocean. As he flew, he had flashbacks of the terrible storm that he had survived by holding onto himself. But since the skies were blue, and the seas calm, his dark memories soon lifted. For a while, he followed in the wake of a school of dolphins. As he passed overhead, he honked, 'If you see your cousin Danny in the north, tell him Gulliver says hello.'

As Lova predicted, it was dusk by the time the coastal mountains loomed on the horizon. Despite his fatigue, Gulliver felt the excitement rising in his chest. His adopted flock could not be too far away now. He wondered how they were coping without him. 'Don't be so silly and arrogant,' Gulliver chastised himself. 'They coped fine without you before and they will cope fine without you again.' He landed safely and found a sheltered spot for the night.

The next morning, Gulliver woke to the sound of something peck-peck-pecking on the ground near him. When he opened his eyes, he was face to face with a bald-headed bird with enormous eyes. The eyes were perched on a scrawny neck, long and rubbery as a snake, and an enormous body covered in luxuriant plumage, supported on tall legs like sapling trees. 'It's a bird,' thought Gulliver groggily – 'but like no bird I've ever seen before.' Gulliver guessed he was in no immediate danger. The bird's beak, although sharp and pointy, did not have the hooked shape of raptors.

'Oscar is my name. Swaziland is my domain. Feathers are my fame. Peering is my game.' He cocked his head, peered more intently into Gulliver's eyes and smiled a broad toothless smile.

A rhyming bird, tall as an elephant? Maybe he was still dreaming! Gulliver shook himself awake and introduced himself, opting to cut his long story short. 'I am a travelling goose named Gulliver, on my way to the Fairest Cape. I was blown off course to Madagascar by a storm and I lost my flock. Now I have returned to find them.'

Oscar's eyes grew big with surprise. But he said nothing. He just went back to pecking on the ground. Gulliver thought this was a bit rude. Then again, Gulliver hadn't asked him a question, nor had he even bothered to find out anything about him. Maybe he was the rude one. So he tried again. 'I am not surprised you are famous for your feathers. You must be able to touch the very edge of heaven with such plush plumes.'

Oscar's eyes welled with tears. Still, he said nothing. Peck. Peck. Peck. Gulliver couldn't imagine how he had offended the giant bird. Surely it was a compliment to be praised as a leader of the open skies? He tried to repair the damage. 'I'm sorry, did I say something wrong? I didn't mean to hurt your feelings. Why are you upset?'

'You ask me why?' replied Oscar, gazing intently at Gulliver. 'Why do I cry? It is because I try. But I cannot fly. I'll never know the sky.'

Gulliver was shocked. Then he thought he understood. 'Did you break a wing? Wings can heal, you know. My friend was shot in her wing and she recovered. It just takes time.'

Oscar shook his head, slowly and sadly. 'No, my little friend,' he said, now too forlorn to even attempt a rhyme. 'My wing is not broken. I am too heavy. None of us ostriches can fly. Our wings are too small for our big bodies. We are cursed by the Sky Gods to peck in the dust all our lives.'

Gulliver was shocked. A bird that cannot fly? How can that be? It seemed so unfair. He didn't know what to say to comfort Oscar. The big bird had turned his back to hide his tears. Peck. Peck. Peck.

Gulliver imagined how helpless Oscar must feel. Almost like he had felt during the storm. He recalled how he had found strength by holding onto himself, but he couldn't tell Oscar that. It wouldn't solve anything. Unless ...

Peck. Peck. Peck.

Gulliver remembered his insight about looking for answers. They were not to be found in the world outside. Answers to the most difficult questions always lie within yourself. Oscar would never be able to fly in this physical world. That much was clear. But maybe he could still find wings within himself. If the body can't fly, maybe the mind can.

Peck. Peck. Peck.

Gulliver closed his eyes and experimented. He imagined taking off and soaring, feeling the wind in his face, flapping his wings and honking to the flock. He was there. It was no different. It was just as real in his mind. Gulliver decided to share the experiment with his dejected new friend. 'My dear Oscar. I realise you are sad. But please indulge me. I want us to play a little game.'

Oscar looked at him. He did not say *yes*. But he did not say *no* either, so Gulliver continued. 'In this game, I need you to close your eyes.' To his delight, Gulliver saw Oscar's eyes close. 'Good. Now imagine you are running, as fast as those powerful legs can take you.' Gulliver noticed Oscar's large toes twitching. 'You are running towards a cliff, but you are not scared. Remember, this is just pretend. Keep running, right over the cliff.' Toes still twitching. 'You expect to fall, but instead a gust of wind lifts you up. You flap your wings and discover you can really fly.' Oscar's wing feathers showed the tiniest ripple of movement. 'You are lighter than air. Feel the breeze on your face. See how the earth stretches out beneath you. Tell me what it's like.'

Without hesitation, Oscar spoke excitedly, once again forgetting to rhyme his words. 'I . . . I can see the patchwork land below, a quilt of greens and browns. I can taste the salt in the air. I can smell a sweet scent of honeysuckle. I can hear my wings beating.'

Gulliver encouraged him on. 'Go higher, Oscar. Higher and further.' Oscar swayed and twitched and clicked his beak. He smiled and laughed and gabbled about all that he was seeing. When Gulliver could see that Oscar had journeyed to the blue horizon in his mind and back, he said, 'And now, make a perfect landing on this highland plateau.'

A few seconds later, Oscar's eyes popped open, wider than ever. He was crying again, but with pure tears of joy. 'I flew! Is it true? I flew! Who knew?'

Gulliver nodded and hugged the long neck of his happy friend. 'You did fly, Oscar! What's more, you can fly again – and again and again – any time you want, for as long as you want.'

Oscar was shaking his head in wonder. 'For so long, we ostriches have been locked in the prison of our bodies. Our whole identity – who we are and how we see ourselves – has been shackled by the belief that we cannot fly. We were always the giant flightless birds. But you have shown me that if we change our beliefs, we can change our world. If we can imagine flying, then we are no longer flightless.'

Oscar was breathless with excitement and bubbling over with new insights. Gulliver was happy for him, but could not shake his own feelings of longing to be back with his adopted flock. Without thinking, he murmured, 'Flying is a great and wondrous thing. But it is even better when you are flying together, instead of alone. A goose without his flock is like a feather without its wing.'

Oscar looked at him queerly, blinked, pecked and looked at him again. Then he said, 'There was a flock that flew. To the south, that's true. And they spoke of you. Honking from the blue: "Gulliver, where are you?"'

Gulliver's heart leapt. Oscar had seen his flock! They must have continued the migration without him. Gulliver's joy was mixed with sadness. Why had nobody waited for him in Zimbabwe? Perhaps they didn't need him after all. Then again, they *were* looking for him. And this place, Swaziland, was south east of where they had been in the House of Stones. The storm could just as easily have blown him here.

As Gulliver wrestled to-and-fro with his feelings, Oscar added, almost as an afterthought. 'One stopped along the way. Name of Gwen, I'd say. Gave me a message that day.'

Gulliver could not believe it. Gwen? His heart was pounding. 'What message? What did she say?'

Peck. Peck. Peck. Gulliver was beginning to realise that pecking on the ground helped Oscar to formulate his thoughts. After a pause, he fixed Gulliver with a stare. 'She said, make no mistake: "If you see a handsome drake. Maybe blown out of shape. Send him on to the Cape. Say that's where we'll wait."'

Gulliver felt a warm, blushing glow rise up to his face, but Oscar did not seem to notice. 'This message gives me hope. You have given me such a gift, Oscar. Thank you, thank you, thank you.' Gulliver was kissing Oscar on the cheek, much to his surprise.

Peck. Peck. Peck.

'I have new hope too, you see,' Oscar replied. 'Such a gift you have given *me*. With your words, you have set me free. With your mind, you were able to lead.'

Gulliver nodded and was about to say his goodbyes. But Oscar was not quite finished yet. 'Now I know the truth, it rings,' he exclaimed with a flourish. 'To fly the highest, you must clip your wings.'

Unconventional Leadership Lesson #12

TO LEARN HOW TO LEAD, YOU MUST FORGET WHAT YOU KNOW

Gulliver thanked Oscar for this new insight and said his farewells. In truth his mind was already chasing the blue – towards the Cape, towards the flock, towards Gwen. The cool, salty sea breeze, which Gulliver breathed in deeply, spread like a fuel injection to the tips of his wings. As the miles sped by, the green dragon mountains rose up on his right and the blue Indian ocean stretched out to his left. Gulliver tried to think about all the great leadership lessons he had learned on his adventures. He tried to remember what Oscar had said about wings and flight. But instead, his tiny brain was filled with the echo of other words, going round and round: 'a handsome drake . . . blown out of shape . . . on to the Cape . . . where we will wait.'

The repetitive mind-loop had the effect of a hypnotic mantra. In what seemed like no time at all, Gulliver noticed the coastline curving dramatically. In fact, he could swear he was now heading more west than south-west. Gulliver sensed that he must be close to his destination, but he didn't know what he was looking for. Suddenly, he was struck by a horrible thought: What if he overshot the place where the flock were waiting? As the chill of dread crept up his spine, he noticed a finger of land jutting out in the distance. When he got closer, he could see a line of froth, where the sea currents appeared to meet. Gulliver flew on, his excitement tussling with his fear and slowly gaining the upper hand. As his spirit lifted, so the mountains rose up alongside the coast in giant folds.

Soon the rocky shore merged into stunning white beaches and the sharp mountains morphed into two hills. The shape reminded Gulliver of his friend Lionel reclining after lunch, although the silhouetted 'face' was more like Cuthbert's. Gulliver decided that this was probably a good place to rest and figure out how to get to the Fairest Cape. A little way off the coast, he spotted a small island, which provided a perfect place to land and consider his options. He also needed to stock up on fuel, after his long journey. Luckily, the rough, shelly island beach was draped in seaweed and algae. Once Gulliver had eaten his fill, he began his post-flight preening routine, while gazing back at the mainland, just as the sun was setting.

Suddenly Gulliver felt all alone. He was overwhelmed by the beautiful spectacle before him – and yet he had no one to share it with. He wondered how he could possibly describe the idyllic scene to his family, or the flock, when he saw them. The lion-camel hills had become indistinguishable against the slopes of a much higher, yet strangely flat-topped mountain. Red and orange tinged clouds were spilling over the mountain's edge, looking for all the world like a tablecloth at a human picnic. At its base, a vast forest of buildings extended to the shoreline of a curving bay. It was easily the most exquisite sight Gulliver had ever seen; certainly the fairest ... Gulliver's walnut brain froze. 'Fairest?' he thought. Electric sparks jumpstarted his synapses. As in, the 'Fairest . . . coastline?'

'The Fairest Cape!' Fireworks exploded in Gulliver's mind. Unable to contain his jubilation, he leapt straight up in the air, flapping his wings wildly and honking with all his might. He had made it! His unexpected journey was at an end. He had successfully migrated. More exciting still, this is where the flock said they would wait. More to the point, this is where Gwen would be. Gulliver spun around, expecting to see the flock, snuck up behind him. But there was no one. He was utterly alone. Maybe they were on the mainland? Gulliver strained his eyes in the fading light, but could not see anything resembling the flock. He strained his ears, but could not hear anything like a honk; only the screech of sea gulls. Gulliver's heart sank.

Suddenly, it was all too much. Getting lost, missing his family, nearly getting shot, almost losing Gwen, getting separated from the flock, nearly dying in the storm, and now this: no joyous honks to welcome him. No golden eyes to gaze into. No nothing. Just the dark shadow of solitude.

Gulliver stood motionless for a moment. Then he started to cry. Mournful weeping gave way to bitter sobs. Soon, Gulliver's tiny bird frame was wracked with convulsions. He had had enough. He was tired. He was fed-up. He was angry. He was deeply unhappy. He didn't care anymore – not about the great migration; not about leadership lessons; not about the flock; and especially not about himself. He may as well just give up and . . .

Gulliver never finished his kamikaze thought-spiral, because just then, the rock he had landed on (after his celebratory leap) started moving. Gulliver squawked and rose up vertically into the air once more, this time from pure fright, landing a few feet away in a fluster of feathers. In a flash of clarity, Gulliver realised that his mind had blown a fuse. His nut brain must have finally cracked under the pressure – because not only had the rock moved, but now it was talking. Suddenly, a wavy image floated before Gulliver's dazed inner eyes – it was mad Goggly, the Scoraig goose that he and his young friends used to tease endlessly as 'the goose with the nut loose.'

As the image of Goggly faded, the words from the talking stone gradually settled and soaked into Gulliver's all-too-porous noggin. 'I'm no expert on these matters, but I find that when life's circumstances overwhelm one, it helps to change them.'

Gulliver, who still could not believe his eyes or ears, only managed to splutter, 'What the pluck . . . '.

After a ponderous pause, the beige and brown stone slowly moved towards Gulliver and continued. 'What I think I mean, or at least what I mean to think, is: If you're not happy where you are, then it's probably a good idea to keep moving.'

Gulliver shook his head, half in disagreement and half in disbelief that he was having a conversation with a rock, albeit a beautifully shaped, prettily patterned rock. He was in no mood for diplomacy, not even with his schizophrenic alter-ego, so he retorted: 'Moving is what got me into this mess in the first place. Moving is what I've been doing for the past six weeks. Moving is precisely why I am unhappy.'

Gulliver was ready for an argument. Instead, the rock grew a head and a neck, which seemed to nod before stretching to nibble on a ribbon of nearby seaweed. After a long pause, the head looked up – it reminded Gulliver of a lizard, except its little mouth was rather beakish. 'Right you are. Very well. Indeed. My mistake. It's just that . . .
,

'It's just that *what!?*' Gulliver was growing impatient with this imagined rock-lizard-bird-creature.'

The scaly face and wrinkled neck, which seemed somehow ancient and wise, was apparently unperturbed by Gulliver's outburst. 'It's just that you seemed to be looking – without success one might add – for something, or someone. Which probably means that that something or someone is not here, in this precise spot. Which seems to suggest that you should move somewhere else, to increase the probability of finding that something, or someone.'

Gulliver opened his mouth to disagree, but couldn't find anything to disagree with, so he shut it again. The black beady eyes of the stone-being were still staring at him, although, it seemed to Gulliver, not unkindly. Before he could think of something mildly intelligent to say to his hallucination, it was speaking again, in a thin, reedy voice. 'My name is Thandi, of the leopard tortoise tribe. If I may be so bold to ask, who might one be speaking to?'

Suddenly, Gulliver knew that this Thandi was not a figment of his imagination. Her shape was all too familiar, as if they had met before, in a different place, a different time. In a blinding flash, Gulliver recalled the vicious snapping turtle from his childhood, clear and terrifying. Once again, he froze, afraid for his life, barely managing to stammer, 'T t t tortoise? Like t t t turtle?'

To Gulliver's surprise, Thandi smiled and chuckled gently. 'Yes and no. Turtles are one's distant cousins, but they swim and they are, dare one say, rather much more feisty and carnivorous. We tortoises, on the other hand, prefer terra firma and delicacies of the herbivorous kind.'

Gulliver had no idea what Thandi had just said, but she seemed quite the opposite of threatening or dangerous. In fact, she seemed to move as slowly, deliberately and gently as she talked. At the first sign of trouble, Gulliver was convinced he could outrun her, not to mention outfly her. That being the case, Gulliver relaxed a little and belatedly remembered his manners. 'Forgive my rudeness. My name is Gulliver. And I am indeed looking for someone – actually more than one – my flock, which I lost in a storm.'

It took very little encouragement from the attentive, patient Thandi for Gulliver to tell her of his travels through Africa and his eventual - and indeed current – isolation. 'The worst part,' Gulliver concluded, still unable to shake off his gloomy mood. 'Is that I'm none the wiser.'

'One finds that hard to believe,' said Thandi sagely. 'Did you not mention certain leadership lessons learned from your new and dear friends?'

'I did,' nodded Gulliver soberly. 'But none of them seems to fit now. Being lost hasn't helped me find the flock. And following myself hasn't led me back to them. I've tried closing my eyes, and walking away and standing in one place. And front or behind or forward or circles mean nothing when you're alone. I can't see how silence or letting go of the past or knowing my roots will get me any closer to finding the flock either.'

Thandi was smiling and chuckling again. 'Right you are. Very well. Indeed. That may be true. But if you would indulge one, one will tell you a story.'

Gulliver was at his wits end. He had nowhere to go and nothing to lose. So he just nodded and slumped down to listen to Thandi's tale.

'There was once a great race around this very island. Believe it or not, it all began when my great grandfather, Thambo, discovered a baby carrot growing in a secret place. Every day, he returned to the spot to check on its progress. Finally, when it was fully grown, my great grandfather decided to give it to my great grandmother, Thuli, as a surprise on her birthday. Unfortunately, a curious and cunning hare named Herman had discovered the same juicy treasure on that very day.'

"What's a hare?' asked Gulliver, nonplussed.

'A kind of African rabbit,' explained Thandi patiently. She took a slow breath, nibbled on some more seaweed and continued. 'Needless to say, my tata Thambo challenged hasty Herman to a race. Whoever won would get to take home the succulent carrot.'

'That's crazy!' exclaimed Gulliver, unable to help himself. 'Why would he make such a bet? Your great grandfather didn't stand a chance.'

'Right you are. Indeed. That's precisely what everyone on the island – and especially Herman – thought. And precisely that many on the island – including the very same Herman – were exactly wrong. In point of fact, my great grandfather Thambo won the race and he and Thuli enjoyed a scrumptious birthday carrot that very evening.'

'How is that even possible?' frowned Gulliver. 'Surely hares, like rabbits, are much, *much* faster than tortoises – no offense intended.'

'Right you are. Indeed. None taken. To be sure, that is the very first lesson one learns as a young tortoise – about being the slowest creature on earth. And many other lessons besides – about defence being the best attack, and about home being wherever you stop to rest. Fortunately for my great grandfather, he was rather forgetful. It so happens that he didn't remember a single lesson of tortoise-lore that he had been taught.'

'I'm not sure I understand,' muttered Gulliver.

'Right you are. Very well. You see, tata Thambo forgot that being slow mattered in a race. He also forgot about going into his shell in defence. He even forgot about stopping to rest. Herman, on the other hand, remembered all his childhood lessons about being quick and clever and savvy. And to show everyone how fast he was, he raced here and there, stopping to chat, helping with chores, delivering messages and playing games. Meanwhile tata Thambo plodded around the island and over the finish line, beating the hapless Herman by a single blink of an eye.'

Gulliver was flabbergasted. It was an amazing story. But he still couldn't quite see how it applied to him and the flock and Gwen.

Thandi noted his confusion and quietly prompted him. 'When the odds were against my great grandfather – as, it would seem, they appear to be against you right now – he did the opposite of what he had been taught to do. I'm no expert on these matters, but perhaps one such as your fine self might try the same?'

Gulliver was willing to try anything at this stage. And so he thought about everything he had learned from his wonderful friends. And then he unthought each leadership lesson, one by one. When he was finished unthinking and unlearning, he was left with a single, simple idea: 'Stop. Looking.' It was the silliest idea he had ever had. But the effort of conjuring it from the nothing left behind had left Gulliver totally exhausted and he fell into a black, dreamless sleep.

The next morning, as a bright yellow sun rose over the placid blue-green bay and waves lapped the island shore, Gulliver woke to the sweetest sound in the world. Honking! Hopeful, happy honking. The flock was silhouetted against the bright morning sky – spearheaded by the unmistakeable sleek form of Gwen. Gulliver's heart beat faster. Raising his face to the sun, he honked loudly. In perfect unison, the flock banked towards him.

Out of the corner of his eye, Gulliver glimpsed Thandi, slowly plodding away. 'Thank you!' he cried. 'I will never forget you, my wise, wonderful friend. I was lost, but now I am found. I am still young and have a lot to learn about being a leader. But I will always remember what you taught me: the biggest lesson in leadership is to forget what one knows.'

The flock landed all around him in happy chaos. Gulliver searched their excited faces until he found one face in particular – with golden eyes that shined brighter than the African sun. And as he and Gwen embraced – lost in love – amidst the cacophony, Gulliver could faintly hear a reedy voice floating on the gentle breeze:

'Right you are. Indeed. Very well. Jolly marvellous.'

~ THE END ~

www.ingramcontent.com/pod-product-compliance
Lightning Source LLC
Chambersburg PA
CBHW071328130626
46556CB00004B/1795